FATED TO THE ALIEN HUNTER

WARRIORS OF TAVIKH
BOOK TWO

ERIN HALE

Fated to the Alien Hunter
© 2023 by Erin Hale
Cover design by Natasha Snow

All Rights Reserved.

No part of this book, with the exception of brief quotations for book reviews or critical articles, may be reproduced or transmitted in any form or by any means, electronic or mechanical, including photocopying, recording, or by any information storage and retrieval system without express written permission from the author. This book may not be used in any way to train any AI.

This is a work of fiction. Names, characters, places, and incidents are the product of the author's imagination or are used fictitiously, and any resemblance to actual persons, living or dead, business establishments, events, or locales is entirely coincidental.

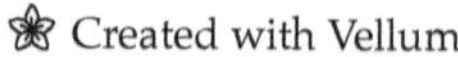 Created with Vellum

CONTENT WARNINGS

As someone who doesn't have any triggers, it is often hard for me to know what might be a trigger for others. I have done my best to include what I think could potentially be triggering for someone. If I have not included yours, I apologize and hope you reach out so I know for the future.

Death of animals from hunting
Violence

CHAPTER I

Zydon

Dust kicks up from the ground of the training arena as Jodah and I spar. He grows tired but continues on the offensive. I jerk my wooden staff above my head to deflect his blow. Vibrations travel down the weapon and into my hands, and where a lesser-skilled fighter might lose their grip and drop it, I maintain a solid hold. I've been sparring with my brothers and Benham since we were kits, and I am five cold seasons older than Jodah, so I've had far more practice. But his skills improve with each turn of the sun.

An opening presents itself, and with a primal snarl, it is my turn to attack. I deliver one punishing strike after another, forcing him backwards until the slightest of stumbles another warrior might have missed, allows me to sweep his feet out from beneath him. A larger cloud of dust rises around his body.

"Well done." I reach to help him up, but a gust of wind brings with it the scent of a trendafili bud. My head snaps up, and my eyes lock onto one of the human females standing at the top of the hill. In an instant, I recognize her.

She stares straight at me as well, and something inside me shifts. But then she whirls away, gone from my sight. Pushing her from my mind, my attention returns to Jodah who's studying me. He finally takes my hand with a slight grin, and I bring him to his feet.

"What was your mistake that allowed me to take you down?" This has been our routine. I defeat him, and then we discuss how to improve his technique and correct the error to make him a better warrior.

"I was distracted by something and took my eyes off you, although it was only for a single beat of my heart."

I nod. "You must never take your eyes off your opponent, and instead, use your ears to listen to your surroundings as well as your instincts to gauge if there is another enemy approaching."

"It would appear Benham was wrong," Jodah says with another grin. "You are not getting too old to spar with the younger warriors."

"He will regret those words when he meets me down here for a training session. We shall see which of us is too old. Now come." I clap him on the shoulder. "Let us head up for the morning meal so you can restore your energy after that bitter defeat."

He laughs as I intend, and we make our way toward the central fire with the rest of the warriors who have finished their own sparring sessions. Several elders are serving bowls of kokrra. It is one of my favorite things, especially sweetened with nectar from the leaves of the shurup plant. It is a meal my nene served when Zander, Zedam, and I were young kits. The scent of it always reminds me of her warmth.

Jodah and I approach with our bowls and stand behind several warriors waiting in a line. He leans forward, and when he does, *she* is there, seated with her tribe sisters and eating her meal. As though sensing my stare, she turns my way, but the moment her eyes meet mine, she dips her head and glances away. I move forward in the line and my gaze is continuously drawn to her. Each time, her gaze meets mine, and each time, she quickly turns.

The human females fascinate me. Or rather, that one in particular does. No one has been happier for Zander than me since he found his human *keeshla*, but it's also a reminder of what many of us don't have. There hasn't been another fated-mates pairing amongst our people in ten cold seasons. However, with the arrival of the females, there's been a new sense of hope for the unmated males that Deeka will bless them with a mate.

I'll admit to feeling it as well. But I quickly dismiss it. A mate isn't for me. Especially not a human one.

After the Krijese attacked their settlement five turns of the sun ago, Zander invited any human who wished to join our village to do so. Along with his mate and her four tribe sisters, several families with kits and a few others arrived. The rest of the humans chose not to come.

I don't agree with Zander's decision to bring them to our village. They expect us to not only provide for them—rather than help themselves or other tribe members—but also protect them. They can't be bothered to learn how to protect themselves. So we've been doing it since they first arrived many lunar cycles ago, and yet they still scorn us and treat us with disdain. As though we are beneath them. *The shefira and her tribe sisters are not like this,* a voice that sounds distinctly like my missing younger brother whispers inside my head.

"You are staring at the female again," Jodah reminds me.

I jerk my gaze away from her and turn to the warrior at my side. He watches me with a smirk. "I'm not staring. Merely observing them."

He grunts and returns to his meal. I do the same, yet my eyes continue to drift to the female with hair the color of the fiku trees. She's the one that walked straight up to Zander and told him she would be training with the warriors. I have not seen her fight yet, but Benham has said what she lacks in skill, she makes up for with determination. I understand she has been rapidly improving.

Jodah and I finish eating and set our bowls beside the fire to be cleaned. Then, I head for my tent to grab several weapons for my patrol. While there hasn't been a direct attack on the village by the Krijese, tensions have mounted since an emissary came to Zander with a peace treaty offer from their king—which he refused. Not when it did not include the human settlement that remains under Tavikhi protection.

I grab the torch from outside my tent, step inside, and plant it within the ground near the small fire pit. Crossing to the other side of the dwelling, I open my weapons chest. Lying on top is my sword. The one Benham crafted especially for me. It is nearly identical to the ones he made for Zander and Zedam, but with a few slight differences. I gently lift it and set it to the side. After removing several daggers, I bring out the leather wrapped item and carefully peel the cloth back to reveal Zedam's sword.

The one we found without him.

Dried blood had coated the blade, but as I hold it up and study it, the metal shines bright and reflects the torch flame behind me. I've kept it clean and sharpened since the day it was discovered on the ground in a small clearing near the beginning of the warm season. There'd been signs of a fight, but no bodies, including those of any Krijese— whose blood decorated the sword—had been spotted. A search party was sent out, but they returned to the village without any news.

Zander mourns Zedam's death, while I remain stubbornly certain he is still alive. Somewhere. Despite all the evidence otherwise. As gently as I'd uncovered it, I fold the leather back over the blade and return it to the chest. I pick up my own sword, attach it to my hip along with the smaller daggers, grab a wooden staff and the torch, and walk outside.

The sun has crested the horizon, and more tribe members have exited their own tents, including several of the humans. They keep their kits close by and do not allow them near our own. Across the distance, Talek runs out of his dwelling and over to another where he slaps the hide exterior. A second Tavikhi kit rushes out moments later, and the two of them take off toward the central fire for their morning meal.

A small ping plucks at the center of my chest, but I brush it away. Kits require a mate, and since I've accepted the fact Deeka means for me to spend my remaining days alone, I don't waste time thinking of things that will never be.

"Good morning, brother."

Zander strides toward me with his *keeshla* at his side and his tail wrapped around her waist. He always finds some way to touch his mate whenever she's near.

"Morning." I acknowledge London with a fist across my chest. "Shefira."

While I may disagree with the humans being here, I would never show disrespect to either my brother or his mate. He and I may argue in private, but never in public.

Her smile is kind. "Good morning, Zydon."

"Heading out on patrol?" Zander asks, his eyes taking in my weapons.

"Rojtar and I are scouting the forest that borders the field nearest the human settlement."

He nods. "Keep an eye out for any dhembe. Benham has heard reports one was spotted in the area."

"Of course." I fist my chest. "We shall return near the midday meal."

With that, I walk toward the gate that guards the village entrance, where Rojtar waits. As I pass the central fire again, against my will I scan the tribespeople still seated around it, but the dark-haired female is missing. I ignore the disappointment that courses through me. Finally, I reach the gate and the younger warrior guarding it greets me with fist over his chest. I return the salute.

On silent feet, we make our way through the clearing, and then the forest swallows us. It's cool within the canopy of the trees, a sign that the cold season is approaching. My vision is sharp as I keep watch for any of our enemies. If the Krijese leader decides to attack, I suspect he will do so before the cold dust falls from the sky to settle on the ground.

"What do you think of the human females? Do you think any more of them could be a warrior's *keeshla?*" Rojtar keeps his voice low and soft, but there's no hiding the hint of hope in it.

"Keep your focus on the forest and any potential danger," I scold him lightly even though there is no hint of any danger on the breeze. Only the scent of the surrounding foliage and the creatures it houses. Two mellenje trading mating calls and the scratching of tiny claws under the nearest nenuphar bush are the only sounds to reach my ears.

I am not normally opposed to occasional conversation during a patrol, but the topic on every tribe members' lips is the humans and the possibility of more fated-mates pairings. Just because Zander met his *keeshla* among them doesn't mean anyone else will. All my hope and prayers to Deeka are devoted to finding Zedam. I have none to spare for finding a mate.

CHAPTER 2

Remi

Despite the chill in the morning air, sweat pours down my face and stings my eyes. There's no time to wipe it away either. Not when I'm defending against a Tavikhi warrior. Our staffs collide and the vibration travels the length of my arm, nearly causing me to lose my grip on the wooden pole. I dodge the next strike, but a whistle close to my ear tells me it almost connected.

While my sparring partners never use their full strength, they don't go easy on me. I'm still forced to block and defend. I'm swift on my feet, but they're swifter. We're in constant motion, never slowing. Certainly never stopping for me to catch my breath. Which leaves me sucking wind, sweat almost blinding me. The Tavikhi across from me doesn't even appear like he's breathing hard.

Quieting my mind, I focus on what I've learned while watching Rassim spar with other warriors. He favors his left and often leaves a narrow opening at his right side. When he takes another swing, I duck beneath it, spin, and strike, landing a blow to his ribs. He grunts and whirls to face me with a giant grin.

"Excellent job, female."

I preen at the compliment and stand a little straighter. I'm so focused on his words that I miss the sweeping motion he makes, and my legs are knocked out from underneath me. My back hits the ground and the air leaves from my lungs with a *whoosh*. There's a brief moment of panic when I can't pull it back in, until, at last, they inflate, and sweet oxygen fills them.

A shadow looms over me, shielding the sun from my eyes, and a large purple hand appears in my vision. I blink away the dust that settled over my face when I fell and grasp it. Rassim pulls me to my feet with ease.

"You cannot allow distractions to break your concentration, female," he chides, telling me something I already know.

"Sorry."

"Do not be sorry." His voice is kind. "It is a lesson you have learned, and you will work harder to not do it again."

He's right. Every critique that's been sent my way has been done in a way that I hear it every time I spar. Which means I don't make the same mistake twice. Usually.

"Again?" I ask, although I'm exhausted and thirsty from the morning's match.

Rassim shakes his head. "We will break until after the midday meal and then return to the training arena."

Grateful, but not wanting to appear weak, I measure my breaths and hold myself and my staff upright. I shoot back a grin. "That should give you plenty of time to recover from that blow to the ribs."

He barks out a small laugh. "A well-placed one."

I nod in appreciation and—with the staff I'm never without—make my way to the river, swiping the back of my arm across my forehead to clear away the sweat that has slowly started to dry. When I reach it, I squat and splash water over my face and then drink from my cupped hands. It's cold and refreshing and soothes my parched lips. Once I've quenched my thirst, I head back to the tent assigned to Zara, Sage, Maeve, and me to grab some clean clothes so I can bathe.

We've been told to take advantage of being able to do so before the cold season comes and it nearly freezes over. Even the Tavikhi don't care for the cold, but they tolerate it. I'm not sure us humans will be able to. Not with the amount of snow we understand the village can get.

The tent is empty when I get there, so I quickly rifle through the trunk that was given to me to store my things, little that there is. After the Krijese attack on the settlement, the four of us were escorted back to it in the hopes that some of our personal belongings hadn't been destroyed in the raid. I managed to salvage enough clothes to last me four days without having to wash any of it. It was enough.

With clean clothes, a handful of green berries that serve as soap, and my wooden staff, I head downriver from where we get our drinking water to the narrow section designated as the bathing area. Even with my height, I can't touch the bottom if I swim out too far. This area is also guarded by a grouping of nenuphar bushes to afford a little privacy. The blue flowers that sprout from the bushes are slowly falling off, but they'll return when the warm season does.

After several warriors accidentally came upon us women —us humans—bathing one day, we quickly devised a way to signal that the river was currently occupied. I remove my dirty sock, hang it from the nearest branch, and step around to the other side of the bushes. I'll grab it once I'm dressed again and wash it along with its match. Since I only have two pairs, I have to alternate them every couple days so they don't get too ripe smelling.

Glancing around out of caution, I strip out of my sweat-stained clothes and toss them off to the side beside my weapon. With soap berries in hand, I step into the water.

"Fuck, it's cold." If this is what it feels like today, I don't want to imagine what it's going to feel like when the cold season actually hits. Gritting my teeth and shivering, I wade the rest of the way out until the water reaches my shoulders. My nipples are so hard they ache, and my teeth chatter.

Zara and I did a bit of investigating during the first couple days after we arrived and discovered from Rassim's mate, Alanda, that there are only two seasons on Tavikh. The warm season and the cold. Based on what some of the elders said—and some rough calculation—we figured out that the warm season lasts about nine Earth months, while the cold season lasts about three. Time is different on this planet than back home. The days last longer, while the nights are shorter. It's taking some getting used to.

I wish my body would acclimate faster, because my circadian rhythm is fucked.

Barely able to stand being in here much longer, I quickly lather the berries and wash everywhere. I groan, because my hair's next. *God, I don't want to do this.* I take a deep breath, and as I'm about to duck under, a flash of movement in the trees draws my attention. When a single Krijese steps out of the forest, I release all the air from my lungs in a scream that sends the alien birds scattering into the sky.

Backpedaling toward the shore, I reach it and grab my staff. I spin around to get into a defensive position, prepared to fight, but there's no sight of him. My head jerks from side to side as I scan the opposite shoreline, but there's no one there.

Far too many minutes later, there's a loud crash through the bushes to my left as two warriors burst into the small clearing with their weapons unsheathed. One is the same warrior who was with Zander's brother earlier. Jonah? Jodah? He glances at me and his eyes widen. Just as fast, he gives me his back and smacks the other warrior's arm, who does the same.

Oh shit.

I drop my weapon and snatch up my clothes to cover my naked body. My arms cross over my breasts and my hand covers my lady bits to hold the fabric against me.

"Female, are you all right?" Jodah calls over his shoulder, keeping his gaze averted. "What happened?"

Jerked out of my panic, I yank on my clean clothes, which soak up the wetness from my skin, leaving them damp and gross feeling. "I'm dressed."

The two Tavikhi slowly pivot to face me. "Female?"

"There was a Krijese over there." I point in the general direction where he'd been standing.

Jodah and the second warrior share a look.

I stiffen in indignation. "I know what I saw. He was right there. When I screamed, I must have scared him off, because by the time I made it to shore, he was gone."

They both startle and the second warrior holds up a hand. "Our apologies female. We did not mean to make you think we do not believe you. Our worry is how he made it past our scouts to get this close to the village."

What if there *were* no scouts. "Do you think he killed them?"

Jodah glances at his friend and nods. The second warrior spins and takes off at a sprint away from the village. I understand further downriver is a place where a person could cross if need be. I've never really believed in any deity, but I send up a quick prayer to the Tavikhi's goddess, Deeka, that the scouts are still alive.

"Come, female. We should return to the village."

Still a bit spooked, I don't argue, despite the fact my dirty clothes are still dirty. I gather them up—as well as my staff—and follow the warrior.

"My name is Remi, by the way, not female," I grumble.

Jodah glances at me. "My apologies, fe—Remi. I am Jodah."

I acknowledge his apology and we walk a bit more in silence. *Don't ask about Zander's brother.*

Before I have a chance to do something stupid, we reach the village. Tavikhi children chase each other around the tents, their adorable little tails slapping behind them. There's no sign of any human children. I'm annoyed at their parents' hypocrisy. The Tavikhi are good enough when they're protecting them within the settlement, but the minute they offer sanctuary in their own home, it's as though being near the Tavikhi will taint them in some way.

We come to a stop in front of the women's sleeping tent. "Thank you for the escort."

"My honor." Jodah crosses his fist over his chest and heads in the direction of Zander and London's tent.

As the chief—or Shefir as the Tavikhi call him—of the entire village, Zander's going to want to know how close one of the Krijese got to it. I step inside our shelter and shudder picturing his thick, rope-like hair and those beady, black eyes that stared at me a bit too intently. The vertical slit of his mouth had been open a fraction and I caught a glimpse of the razor-sharp teeth hidden behind it. The up-close-and-personal look I got at one the night of the attack when he grabbed Sage and I beat him with my staff is more than enough for me.

I set my dirty clothes on top of the chest. I'll wash them tomorrow. When I won't be alone. And since there's nothing to do until after the midday meal when Rassim and I spar again, I head out in search of my friends.

CHAPTER 3

Zydon

The forest surrounding us is quiet. Not even our footsteps can be heard. A cold breeze comes from the direction of the hills that house the dhibani. Tomorrow I will head for them for some hunting. With the quickly approaching cold season and the addition of the humans to our tribe, we need to replenish our fur supply. Smoking their meat will also provide food for our stores to help us last until the warm season returns.

"Do you think one of the human females would take the midday meal with me when we return?" Rojtar breaks the silence once again with the topic I've diverted him from since we set off on our patrol.

I bristle. Which female is he interested in? Is it the one with hair similar in color to ours? Perhaps the small one that reminds me of a ketri kit? It can't be Kyler's apprentice.

She has been coming to the village to learn healing for several lunar cycles and he's never indicated any interest in her beyond the mild curiosity we all had when she first arrived. Or is he interested in the warrior female who smells of trendafili?

"Zydon? Is all well?"

My fists unclench from the tight grip I have on my staff. "Of course. Why would it not be?"

Rojtar stares at me with concern. "You were growling like a luani."

I clear my throat. "All is well."

He continues to cast glances in my direction as we close in on the village. The call of a mellenje fills the air and I answer with one of my own. Seconds later, one of our scouts appears from his hiding place high up in the tree. He descends with grace and speed, his tail wrapping around each branch to secure him until he lands on his feet before us.

"Be vigilant up ahead. One of the human females spotted a Krijese on the opposite shore of the bathing spot right after the morning meal."

My tail lashes behind me at the thought it could be *her*. "Which female? Is she hurt?"

He shakes his head. "He did not attack. Merely stood watching her until she scrambled out of the water to retrieve her wooden staff near her discarded clothes. When she turned to defend herself, he was gone."

A sharp emotion stabs at me. It is the one with hair the color of the fiku tree. The warrior.

"Come, let us continue." I salute the scout, who nods and then scrambles back up the tree to return to his post.

Rojtar and I leave him behind and make our way through the remaining section of the forest until we reach the clearing.

"How did a Krijese warrior get that close to the village?" he asks, for once today the topic not about the human females.

"I do not know, which is why we must hurry." I do not admit there might be another reason for our haste.

We focus around us, but the field is empty. Even the small section of fiku trees that lead the way to the gate is empty. The guards at the entrance straighten at our approach and fist their chests. I return the gesture and stride through the village, intent on reaching Zander's hut. Rojtar separates from me and makes his way toward one of the tents a few of the younger warriors share.

I cross the length of the village, my gaze sweeping side to side. The central fire has been stoked and several tribespeople bustle around it preparing the midday meal. There is no sense of urgency. No warriors scurrying about on their way to the weapons stores. A few humans wander around, but not one human in particular. I blow out a breath. Why do I even care about the female? *Because she is a member of this tribe and I care about all our tribespeople*, I tell myself.

I stride toward my brother's home and slap on the door covering, announcing my arrival. No one is inside.

Cursing, I turn and head for my tent, only to find Zander is making his way toward me. I meet him partway.

"How was your patrol?" he asks.

"Uneventful. There were a few human males sparring outside the settlement walls with one of the warriors you assigned to train them." I shake my head. "They are still as unskilled as ever."

He claps me on the shoulder. "It has only been five turns of the sun. We cannot expect them to be warriors yet. They will learn, just as we did. Hunting and fighting are our way of life. We were raised as kits to learn. The humans did not have such a youth. They lived in dwellings stacked so high they nearly touch the sky, with machines that provide them food. If they are lucky."

"And if they are unlucky?"

"My *keeshla* says that the poorest members of the villages must fend for themselves. They have no machines, but rather must barter for nothing more than protein bars to fill their bellies. No one does anything for the good of all. The ones with the most do not share with the ones with the least."

By the goddess, what kind of planet is Earth? Perhaps that is the reason the humans have chosen to come here. They hope for a better life than they had. "I shall work on being more patient and forgiving of them."

"Thank you, brother."

"Now tell me about this Krijese who reached this close to our village. A scout near the gate said he came upon one of the human females bathing."

"Why don't you take your weapons back to your tent and meet me at the central fire? We can discuss it while we eat."

This is the reason Zander makes a better Shefir than I would. He is patient and thinks things through. I, on the other hand, am often impulsive and impatient. Waiting is something I am not skilled at. I nod and try not to rush to my tent. I prop my staff against the hide inside the entrance and then take care with my sword. No matter how impatient I might be, my weapon is my most prized possession and must be treated as such.

At last I finish and exit my tent for the central fire. Various tribespeople, as well as humans, slowly trickle in from different directions. There is still no sign of our shefira and her tribe sisters. Zander has already been served and is seated in his usual place on the large bench made from a fallen fiku tree. I quickly gather my own meal and sit on one side of him since the other side is reserved for his *keeshla*.

I bite my tongue to withhold my questions and instead eat. All while I keep scanning the area. Finally, Zander pauses his meal.

"The humans can no longer go to the bathing area unless a warrior accompanies them. They will continue to have their privacy, but whoever is assigned that day will remain close by."

"How did the Krijese make it through our scouts? Or did he kill them?"

Zander shakes his head. His expression is the one that says he's deep in thought. "That is what I do not understand. Both scouts were knocked unconscious, but otherwise unharmed. He also did nothing more than stand at the edge of the forest. Remi said he made no moves of aggression."

Remi. I swirl it around inside my head. So that is the name of the human female warrior.

"Does this mean that King Armik has agreed to your terms of the peaceful truce between our peoples to include the human settlement as well?" When Zander made this demand to the king's emissary, he became enraged.

"It is too soon to tell. There has been no word of any more raids on the settlement in five turns of the sun. But the Krijese lost many of their males during their last attack. Perhaps the king is merely biding his time. Waiting until he thinks we, along with the humans, have let our guard down. Then he will strike."

"We must never let down our guard then."

Zander glances at me. "It is an exhausting endeavor, is it not? Always remaining on guard? Always having to worry about our people? It's the one thing that weighed the heaviest on Baba when he was Shefir."

"And yet we will continue to do so, not only because you —the shefir we trust to do what's best—ask it of us, but because we all care about protecting our tribespeople." I do not envy my brother, nor our baba before him, for his role in our village, having to make decisions that affect us all.

He claps my shoulder and then his gaze shifts past me. His pupils flare and his tail swishes behind him. I turn toward whatever has caught his attention, although based on his reaction the answer is obvious. Gathered with her tribe sisters and heading this way is his *keeshla*. I only spare her a single glance before my gaze latches onto the female nearest her. Onto *Remi*.

She and the three others branch off and make for the central fire. My eyes remain on her until Zander crosses in front of me and I lose sight. London walks into his arms, and he bends to press his mouth to hers and twine his tail around her leg. I have witnessed this mouth touching between them before. He says it is called kissing.

An image of Remi's face appears in my mind. I try to imagine what her lips would feel like. Soft like the petals of the flowers of the nenuphar bush? Rough like leburin hide after it has gotten wet? Annoyed with myself, I wipe all thoughts of mouth touching from my mind. What her lips feel like does not matter. Neither this kissing nor mating are for me.

CHAPTER 4

Hours after my bathing experience, I'm still a bit jittery. I keep waiting for the alarms to sound and the Krijese to attack. But all day it's been business as usual around the village.

"Don't look now, but your boyfriend is staring again." Zara nudges me as we help ourselves to the stew in the large clay pot balanced over the cook fire.

What do I do? I look.

Remington Alcott always did what she was told and never would have looked. Remi, on the other hand, balks against commands. Even ones that are good for her. Sure enough, my eyes meet the bright-yellow feline ones of Zander's brother. Who he will remain, because using his name feels too…intimate. Too much like a real man—alien—instead of just someone vaguely associated with the shefir. An alien who *doesn't* make the hair stand up on my arms.

"He's not my boyfriend," I say weakly after far too long a delay.

"I don't know," Sage points out over the top of Maeve who stands between us. "Zydon has been paying a lot of attention to you since we got here while trying to make it look like he's not paying attention to you."

"It doesn't matter if he pays attention or doesn't. I'm not interested." I'm *not*. "All my focus is on my training. I don't need any distractions. Especially of the male variety."

"I wouldn't mind some distraction," Sage says with a wiggle up and down of her eyebrows.

Maeve rolls her shoulders forward and dips her head like she does whenever she's uncomfortable. I give a pointed stare at Sage and Zara and discreetly tilt my head toward our quiet friend. They both glance at Maeve with sympathy and mouth 'sorry' to me. None of us know her story or what made her choose to come to Tavikh. In fact, I'm not sure we even know London's or Sage's either.

"Not to change the subject or anything," Zara speaks up, doing precisely that. "But I spent the time since the morning meal, and since the elders kicked me out of the tanning tent, strolling around the village observing everything."

The four of us all take our food bowls and find a seat on one of the benches that flank the central fire. As usual,

Maeve sits on the ground between us, tucked in close to our legs. She always declines a seat next to us, so we've stopped pushing.

"And?" I prompt when Zara leaves us hanging. "Find anything special?"

"I'm not sure. Or at least I don't want to get my hopes up."

"About what?" Sage asks before taking a bite of stew.

Maeve peers up at us with wide eyes too big for her face, waiting for whatever it is that Zara thinks she found.

"One of the warriors—the big, grumpy one—is apparently the village weapon maker," Zara finally spits out. "He's the one who makes all the warrior's swords and daggers. Anyway, I watched him work for a while today, and it was fascinating. It's actually the first thing that's even remotely struck my interest since we landed on this planet."

We all gape at her. Even Maeve, who's always the first to offer a sweet and soft pep talk to one of us. I'm the first to snap out of it.

"You want to make weapons?" I ask, still slightly skeptical.

Zara shrugs a bit self-consciously and I instantly feel bad, because I know how difficult adjusting to this place has been for her.

"Hey." I reach out and lay my hand on her arm. "If you think it's something you might like, then I think you should do it."

"Yeah," Sage encourages.

"I bet you'll be really good at it," Maeve says quietly touching Zara's knee.

She snorts. "I don't know about being good at it, but I can't be any worse at it than I was at cooking."

We all groan—the stench of burnt leburin stew still burns our noses days later from the one and only time the tribespeople let Zara try her hand at preparing a meal.

"You're going to be great." I shoulder bump her and try to infuse as much positivity into my tone as I can without sounding insincere.

"The only challenge I foresee is getting Benham to agree to it," Sage notes. "He's not particularly fond of humans."

Zara straightens and raises her chin. "He just hasn't met me yet. I'm one of the most likeable people there is besides you three and London. Besides, Benham doesn't have to like me. He just has to tolerate me and teach me how to do what he does."

She's not wrong about that. She's fun and friendly and always the first person to try and cheer someone up when they're down. I suppose if anyone can make a good impression on the grumpy warrior, it's her.

"Good luck," I wish her. *You're probably going to need it.*

We finish eating and return our bowls to the stack to be washed.

"Do you guys want to go back to the tent for a little while and play Pebbles?" Zara asks.

Sage shakes her head. "Sorry, I need to head back to the medicine tent. One of the warriors injured during the attack on the settlement needs his wound checked and rebandaged. Plus, I'm working on making a new cream formula for us humans. I don't know about you, but my skin gets chapped in the winter, and there's not much here in the way of skin protection. So I'm making some. Or at least trying to."

"Yeah, and I need to meet Rassim soon for our next training session," I tell her.

Zara glances down at Maeve, who winces. "I told Alanda I would help her harvest some of the roots and spices after the midday meal."

"Maybe this is the perfect opportunity for you to approach Benham about becoming an apprentice," Sage suggests with a tip of her chin. "He looks like he's in a reasonable mood."

We all glance in that direction where the warrior in question stands at the edge of the central circle speaking to another tribesman. *That's* his reasonable appearance? He towers over the other male—who already stands close to seven feet—and is significantly bulkier. Not fat, but solid. Scars cover his arms and there's one along the side of his face that disappears into his hairline. What's most off-putting about him though is the scowl that never leaves his face.

I turn to Zara who takes a deep breath and stands. She squares her shoulders and strides confidently forward. Of all of us, she's the one who hides her self-consciousness the best. She comes to a stop within feet of the two warriors who both stare down at her. Her back is to us, so none of us can see her face or what she's saying. The shorter warrior walks away and Benham pivots so he's head on with her and crosses his arms. Even from this distance there's no mistaking the irritation in his eyes.

"Does anyone want to take a bet that he's going to make her cry?" Sage stage whispers.

London, Maeve, and I spent two months on a ship with Zara, while Sage has only known her a handful of days. I shake my head. "Zara is made of much sterner stuff than that. She's pretty fearless. Sometimes to an extreme. I wouldn't bet against her."

"What are you all staring at?" London asks as she takes Zara's spot on the bench and twists at the waist toward where our gazes are all focused.

"Zara's talking to Benham about teaching her how to make weapons," I fill her in.

She whips around to stare. To my complete shock, he hasn't sent Zara away. Instead, the two are still speaking. I try to read his lips, but it's impossible. Finally, he gives a sharp nod and then walks away. She remains standing with her back to us for another few seconds until she, at last, turns with a dazed expression.

Slowly she starts forward, her gaze still unfocused until she blinks and gives her head a small shake. Then Zara lifts her head. Her eyes widen and she almost runs back.

"Oh my god, he said yes," she says the second she reaches us.

We all jump up and squeal our excitement. I give her a huge hug. "I'm so happy for you."

Her happiness stalls out and uncertainty flashes across her face. "What if I'm shit at this too? What if I'm getting excited about this for nothing, because it's one more thing I suck at?"

London gives Zara a stern look. "No talking like that. This is going to work out for you, you'll see. I have a good feeling about this. Benham might be a grouch, but I've watched him with the kits and he's extremely patient with them. He'll be patient with you as well."

Zara gasps with mock affront. "Did you just compare me to a child?"

London sticks out her tongue and everyone laughs. I scoot over to make room for her on the bench, but Zara doesn't take it.

"He wants me to meet him at his forge."

"Now?" I blink.

She nods. "He said I might as well get started. Of course, as he was leaving, I heard him grumble something under his breath about humans. But I'm not going to let his sourness ruin anything. He's probably trying to see if I can handle his cranky ass. Benham doesn't know who he's dealing with yet."

Maeve squeezes Zara's hand. "I have faith in you."

"Aw, thanks Mae."

"I don't mean to break up our little party, but I need to head to the healer's tent," Sage says. "Congratulations, Zara, I'm happy for you."

"Thanks, Sage."

As she walks away, Rassim is heading this way. He comes to a stop before us and glances first at London. He bows his head and lays his fist over his chest. "Greetings, Shefira and her tribe sisters."

London has told us that she's still not quite used to being addressed first when we're all together. I think it's nice that they show her the respect that comes with her new title. Rassim turns to me and grins.

"Are you ready for our training session?"

"Have you recovered from that tap to your ribs?" I smirk.

"I believe I shall make it," he replies with an answering grin.

With all of us having things to take care of, our group breaks away, and each of us heads off in opposite directions. I grab a skin of water from near the fire and take it with me. With that look of mischief in Rassim's gaze, I can already tell I'm going to need it.

CHAPTER 5

ZYDON

Curious about the female's fighting skills, I make my way to the training area where she and Rassim went after the midday meal to observe them. I stand at the top of the hill, not far from where I spotted her this morning, and stare down into the shallow valley. There are several other warrior pairings also sparring. Some use wooden staffs, while others are practicing with capped swords to protect from drawing blood.

She—Remi—twists her hair on top of her head, secures it, and takes position with her staff held firmly in her hands. Rassim is opposite her and in his own defensive stance. They both move at once and their dance begins. Rassim goes on the offensive and their staffs crack together. He jabs with his right arm and Remi blocks it. Back and forth, they trade hits, neither gaining the upper hand.

The female is graceful in her movements and sharply observant. It is clear she has made a note of Rassim's weaknesses and uses them to her advantage. She dodges a blow and lands one of her own to the side he left exposed. He grins and increases the speed in which he attacks. Remi keeps up, but I can sense her tiring. Rassim must as well, because he lunges, and with a sharp upward swipe, he knocks the staff out of her hands. To my shock, she dives, snatches it off the ground as she rolls, and jumps back to her feet.

"She would make a fine mate for a warrior, would she not?"

I startle at the question and also that I missed Zander's approach. If I became this distracted in the middle of a battle, I would be easily defeated. I glance at him and do not miss the calculating look in his eyes.

"If one were looking, perhaps that might be true."

Amusement flits across his face, an emotion I have not witnessed enough since before Zedam went missing. My womb mate became much more serious after our younger brother's disappearance, although his smiles have come a bit easier since his mating with his *keeshla*.

"You forget that I know you as well as I know myself, brother. You are fascinated with the female," Zander announces.

"I am merely observing her fighting skills to see if she is improving as both Benham and Rassim have noted."

He glances down to where the match continues and then returns his gaze to me. "And what are your observations?"

Taking the bait, I go back to studying her. The way her cheeks turn the same color as the petals of the lulebore flower. How strands of her dark hair escape from their confines and brush her pale shoulders, which leads my gaze to take in the rest of her. Unlike our females, the humans possess chest mounds. My fingers twitch with curiosity to discover what they feel like. She does not possess the same curves as our shefira, but Remi is still fully female. Her legs are long and nicely muscled. But I say none of this to Zander.

"She is cautious, but not timid. She also takes advantage of any sign of Rassim's weakness. It is obvious she pays attention to his fighting style and tries to adapt hers to it to a varying degree of success. She's aware of her limitations in regard to strength and uses other methods to make up for it."

"Those are some powerful observations in such a short time," Zander notes.

"*You* seem to forget that I have been training since we were kits. It is my task to quickly learn as much as I can about an opponent."

One of his brow ridges shifts upward. "I did not realize Remi is an opponent."

I turn my gaze away from him and back down to the sparring pair. Just as my eyes land on them, Rassim strikes a blow that Remi is unable to dodge. The female stumbles sideways and falls to the ground. Before I realize what I am doing, I make to charge down there, but Zander slaps his forearm across my chest, stopping me. I whip my head in his direction.

"She will not appreciate your interference."

An unfamiliar anger fills me. Something I am not used to. "So we are meant to stand here and let her—a female—get injured?"

"It is what Remi wants. To be treated as any other warrior. Which means there may be times she suffers a minor injury. Better it be from one of us and when there is a healer available than to be grievously injured by a Krijese." Zander motions toward the arena. "See, she is already rising to her feet."

I turn back to her and find my brother is right. Rassim is speaking to her and there's a brief hesitation before she nods. He picks her weapon up off the ground and passes it over. Remi takes it, and the two of them walk out of the arena and ascend the hill. Her movements are slow, and she is favoring her right leg. They get closer, and pain is etched on her face.

She lifts her head when they reach the top, and at the sight of me, she stumbles slightly. Rassim steadies her and my gaze shifts to where he grips her arm. Not letting him stop me this time, I push past Zander and head for the pair.

"Go see the healer, female," I announce to moment I reach them.

Remi abruptly stops and glares at me. "Excuse me?"

Rassim releases her and takes a step back.

"I said, go see—"

"I heard what you said," she spits out like an angry ketri and resumes her uneven gait away from me.

"Then why did you act as though I needed to repeat it?" I keep pace with her.

Remi shakes her head. "It wasn't a request for you to boss me around again."

"I do not understand what *boss you around* means." Although I have my suspicions.

She glares at me yet again but does not stop, although her limp grows more pronounced. "It means command me. Or make a demand. Take your pick."

"It was not a command." Although perhaps it was.

"Sure sounded like one to me."

"Are all humans this stubborn?"

"Are all Tavikhi this imperious?" Remi waves her finger up and down in my direction.

I narrow my gaze, but she's staring straight ahead and almost stomping. "What is this *imperious*?"

She finally comes to a stop outside a tent and whirls on me. "Arrogant. Demanding. *Rude.*"

Offended at her assumption, I rear back. "I am none of those things."

"Could have fooled me. Now, if you'll excuse me, I am going inside to lie down." With that, Remi jerks open the hide door covering, steps into her tent, and lets it slap closed.

I stare at the entrance for several beats of my heart and finally turn and walk away. What in Deeka's name came over me? I have never spoken to a female like that before. *You have also never had that kind of reaction to a female before.* She is stubborn. Far more than any of the Tavikhi females.

I head for the healer. If she will not go to him, then he will go to her. I enter the next largest tent after Zander's. Three raised platforms stacked with furs fill the space. One of them is occupied with a warrior who'd been injured in the Krijese attack against the human settlement. The healer's human apprentice tends him, but she glances up at my arrival.

"Can I help you?"

"I need a healer," I tell her.

Her gaze travels over me in a clinical way. "What's bothering you?"

"Not me. The warrior female. Remi. She was hurt during her sparring session."

The apprentice leans to the side and her eyes dart behind me before she straightens. "Where is she? Is she bleeding? Did she break something?"

"She is limping and in pain." Why is she asking me all these questions instead of going to help her tribe sister?

Her posture relaxes. She brings the fur covering up over the warrior's bandaged chest and walks to the other side of the tent where several clay jars sit on a high table. "If Remi was hurt more than she could handle, she'd come see Kyler or me."

I shake my head. "She is too stubborn."

The female pauses in whatever task it is she is doing with the jars and glances over at me again. "She's not *that* stubborn."

I stand there a moment longer. Why am I so concerned about this human? I am not. With that decision made, I spin away with my tail thrashing behind me. I need something to take my mind off the female. Perhaps Jodah will meet me in the training arena for a sparring session. Anything to keep me from thinking about the distracting human.

CHAPTER 6

REMI

I'm almost glad everyone is off doing their own thing so I can wallow in misery by myself. But I also wish at least one of my friends was here so I could rant about that pompous jackass. Did he seriously think I was going to jump to his command? Granted, for a brief second, I had considered going to see Sage at the healer's tent, if for nothing more than a small dose of the ground up root she and the healer use for pain.

Except I had too many people in my life back on Earth telling me what to do. There's no way I'm going to let people on Tavikh start doing it as well. Even if that means being called stubborn. If he'd framed it as a concerned suggestion, then I probably would have gone. Instead, I'm going to lie in my bed of furs and will away the pain while

I wait for Sage to get back. I'll see if she'll run and grab me something to help take the edge off.

I prop my staff up against the wall on my side of our tent and slowly lower myself onto my pallet. A small fire burns in the center pit, the orange, yellow, and red flames flickering toward the opening at the top to let the smoke escape. I roll up my pant leg and wince at the giant red mark that, from past experience, will be a black-and-grayish-purple bruise by tomorrow, if not later tonight. Already a portion of the skin is turning colors. I gently touch the area and hiss at the pain that shoots up my leg. Fuck, that hurts.

Ever since we left Earth on the the Exodus Voyager, I have done everything I can to erase who I used to be. It's meant wearing clothes I never would have worn before. Being friends with people my parents never would have approved of. I've pushed myself physically, mentally, and emotionally to try and break all the chains that tie me to Remington Alcott—dutiful daughter of Sinclair and Elizabeth Alcott—and my old life.

Someone slaps on the hide flap that covers the opening into the tent.

"Remi. It is Alanda. May I enter?"

I sit up. "Of course, come in."

She lifts the flap and sunlight shines brightly around her, and then it closes behind her leaving us in only the pale light given off by the fire. She lowers herself to her knees, and in her hands is a small leather pouch that she passes to me.

"Rassim told me you would need this. He thought it better if I brought it to you than if he did."

I open it and a scent similar to eucalyptus, but not quite, rises from inside. Relief and a healthy dose of appreciation well up inside me. "Thank you so much, Alanda. And please tell Rassim thank you as well."

She smiles softly and dips her head. "It is my honor. I am always happy to help our shefira's closest tribe sisters."

"You really are a lifesaver."

Her eyes widen and the catlike vertical pupils dilate. "Rassim did not say you were dying. I will go get the healer."

I sputter a laugh and reach out to clasp her arm. "No, no. I'm not dying. It's just a figure of speech."

Alanda slowly lowers herself back down. "You are sure? According to my translator, you said I saved your life."

"Trust me, you did save it, but not because I'm dying."

She still doesn't look like she believes me, but she doesn't push the topic. "Well, I am glad to be your…lifesaver."

"Thank you. Would you please tell Rassim that I'll meet him before the morning meal tomorrow for another sparring session like usual?" If other warriors can still train with bruises and other minor injuries, then so can I.

"I will tell him." Alanda stands. "If you need any more burim root, let me know."

I jiggle the pouch. "This should be enough, but I appreciate it."

She exits the tent, the sounds of the village growing loud when she opens the flap, then dying down to a muffled buzz. I grab the water skin off the small table within reach and pour a dash of powder in my palm that I toss into my mouth and wash it down with a few swigs of water. I shudder at the leafy, dirty taste, but considering the potency of the pain reliever, I tolerate it. After setting the skin back, I crawl under my furs for a short nap and to let the root take effect. As I feel myself drift off, a pair of dark-yellow eyes, full lips, and a sharp jawline with leathered purple skin follow me into my dreams.

***

"Remi."

I moan and roll over.

"Remi. Wake up," the voice says insistently, and someone pushes against me.

"Unhn." I groan and slowly open my eyes. Zara kneels beside me with her hand on my shoulder. "Wha—I'm awake. What time is it?"

She moves away and sits on her own pallet. "It's almost time for the evening meal. You've been asleep for a few hours. Are you okay? Alanda told London you got hurt training with Rassim earlier."

I swipe my hair out of my face and sit up, slowly moving my leg out as I do. There's still some pain, but it's definitely more muted than it had been before my nap. "I'm fine. Wasn't fast enough to dodge a strike and got a good smack in my leg for the effort. Probably going to have a beauty of a bruise tomorrow."

"I heard you had a small confrontation with your boyfriend." Zara smirks.

"Ugh, don't mention that guy." I'm also annoyed because I had more than one dream about it while I'd been napping. He was far less bossy in them.

"What started it?"

"After Rassim and I got to the top of the hill from the training arena, he was already there and demanding I go to the healer. Didn't ask me if I was okay or anything. Just 'go to the healer,'" I lower my voice trying to imitate his. "You know how I feel about being told what to do. If anyone else knows what it's like, it's you."

Zara and I grew up in a similar type of home, although hers sounded a bit worse than mine. Regardless, we were both raised to obey and follow all kinds of social dictates. It's one reason she's had such a hard time finding her way of contributing to the village. She'd had everything done for her her entire life.

"The freedom we have here is a bit overwhelming, but yeah, being back under someone's rule is not something I would like. Maybe he's one of those guys who acts all demanding and pushy because he cares?"

I gape at her. "Why would Zydon care? He doesn't even know me."

Zara is quiet for a moment. "Have you considered maybe you're his mate, but since he hasn't touched you yet, his marks haven't been triggered? Maybe even *he* doesn't realize you are mates."

From the beginning, I've had a hard time wrapping my head around this whole mate thing. I know that when Zander touched London the first time on the day we landed here, those strange tattoos on his body appeared and turned a dark purple that's nearly black, but it feels like a fluke. A weird coincidence. Does a goddess *really* pick out a person's mate or is it just some weird biological reaction that triggers their marks to appear?

"No, definitely not. Besides, I don't want a mate. Especially *him*. Can you imagine? I escaped one prison already. I have no plans on entering another one. Zydon's already proven how domineering he can be. I bet he'd be a thousand times worse if we were mates."

Zara shrugs. "It was just a suggestion."

I wave it off. "I don't want to talk about Zydon or mates or anything else like that. Why don't you tell me how it went with Benham?"

She looks like she wants to say more on the topic but thankfully leaves it. "I didn't impale myself, burn myself, or catch anything on fire, so I guess it's a start."

I snort. "That's good. Do you think you're going to enjoy apprenticing for him?"

Zara pauses and then nods. "Actually, I think I will. Benham's a bit on the grumpy side, sure, but he was surprisingly patient with me. Even with all the questions I asked. And even after I broke one of the daggers he'd been making when I hit it with a hammer. I braced myself for an explosion of temper, but instead, he explained kindly what I'd done wrong and how to not make the same mistake twice."

"I'm really happy for you, Zar." I am too. We all saw how frustrated she'd been getting 'failing' at everything.

"Are you guys coming to dinner or not?" a voice hollers outside the tent.

"We're coming." Zara and I share a look and she gets up on her feet. "Need a hand?"

"I think I can handle it." Slowly and with care, I test my leg out and stand. I shift to put most of my weight on it and there's a twinge, but it doesn't shoot through my whole leg like it had earlier. After I bounce on it a little and it doesn't give out on me, I figure I'll make it to the central fire. I nod. "Yep, I'm good."

She exits first and I'm right behind her. Sage, Maeve, and, to my surprise, London, are waiting for us.

"I figured you'd be with Zander. He's never far from you."

She sticks her tongue out at me. "You act as though we're attached at the hip."

All of us side-eye her and she laughs. "Okay, fine, so we're together a lot. Just wait until you guys meet your mates and then you'll be together all the time too."

"Not me. I have no intention of mating anyone." I shake my head.

"Me either," Maeve speaks up, although it's still quietly.

Sage and Zara merely shrug. London meets my eyes and she smirks. "You know you jinxed yourself, right?"

"No I didn't. There's no such thing." I've never been a superstitious person.

She latches onto my arm and pulls me toward the central fire. "We'll see."

Her tone makes me uneasy. It's almost like she knows something I don't.

CHAPTER 7

"I don't want a mate. Especially him."

I do not want a mate either, but that Remi thinks a mating between us would be a prison stings like the bite of the mushkanja. Perhaps that is why I cannot get her words out of my mind.

"You are distracted today," Jodah points out. "Is all well?"

"Yes." I tighten my grip on my spear and scan the field of nearly waist-high bari for any sign of our enemies or prey.

"Does it have anything to do with your female?"

I dart a glance at him. "She is not *my* female." Nor does she want to be.

He makes a noise as though he doesn't believe me.

"I don't want a mate."

Shaking my head, I work to dislodge the voice inside it. Not all of us are meant to have a mate anyway. Jodah makes another sound, but this one brings my head up. There, at the far side of the field, is a single dreri. The color of its hide helps it to blend into its surroundings, but the large, dark-colored horns are difficult to hide. Two single horns rise from each side of its head before branching off into several smaller horns that branch off into even smaller ones. Based on the number of times they split, it is definitely male and well into adulthood.

I glance over at Jodah, and he nods. We move slowly in opposite directions to flank the beast and close in. My footsteps are light, and I barely breathe. I don't look at Jodah again. We have hunted together enough times to trust what the other is doing. Instead, I keep my gaze on the dreri that grows bigger the closer we get to it.

It snaps its head up as though sensing predators nearby, and I freeze. When it feels the danger must have passed, it lowers itself to return to its grazing. Finally, when I'm within striking distance, I glance across the distance to Jodah, who's also gotten into position. We both nod in readiness, and together we move as a single hunter.

The dreri jerks to the side and tries to impale me with its deadly horns, but Jodah is there to bring it down with his spear. It stumbles, then falls, and I quickly end its suffering. As Benham does, I offer up a prayer of thanks to the beast for giving its life and to Deeka for providing us with more food we will be able to stock for the coming cold season.

Jodah retrieves his weapon, and I sling the animal across my shoulders and carry it as we travel closer to the hills where the dhibani live. If we can take down at least two of them, then I will call today a success.

"Zydon," Jodah says quietly.

I turn my gaze to him and then to where his focus is directed. At the base of the nearest hill are two figures. They creep along the trail, moving farther away from us. But there's no mistaking the pair of Krijese. What are they doing this far from their village? It is more than a turn of the sun away. Careful not to draw their attention, I sling the dreri off my shoulders and let it fall to the ground.

With a nod, we creep forward. If they choose to fight, we will. Unless this is a trap and more are hiding in the shadowed crevices of the hills, two of our enemy will be unable to defeat us. I keep my spear at the ready, but I itch to withdraw my sword. It's a better weapon to defend myself against an opponent if need be.

We draw closer, our steps light, until a flock of mellenje flies into the air with a cry. The two Krijese spin at the sound and shift into battle position as they each reach for their long-handled ax they favor. As stealth is no longer required, we do not hide our presence.

"We do not want to fight you, Tavikhi," one calls out in their guttural language, straightening and lowering his arm to his side.

Since when? The Tavikhi and Krijese have been warring for countless lunar cycles. Long before Baba was Shefir.

"What are you doing so far from your village?" Jodah calls out.

The two exchange glances, and the first jerks his chin. "There are a small number of us who have left King Armik's village. We no longer want to wage war against your people. All we want is peace."

I don't dare take my eyes off them. "Your people do not know the meaning of peace. You have done nothing but cause destruction."

One shakes his head, the ropes of his hair flaring out around him. "Our people are dying. King Armik hoards our kills for himself, and we are slowly starving. Our females are almost gone. As are our kits. Soon there will be no one left."

"So you have left and created your own village?" I ask.

"Yes. We are only a handful, but there are so few beasts left near our old village that we moved to where the hunt can be more plentiful."

I glance at Jodah. "Do you believe them?"

"What reason do they have to lie? They have the look of one who has not eaten his share in many cycles. If this was a trap, where are the rest of them? Why have they not attacked yet? We would be easily outnumbered despite our superior fighting skills."

His observations are true. There is no one around but these two males. They have not tried to attack us. "If you are lying, we will not hesitate to kill you."

They nod.

Despite their declaration of wanting peace, I do not want to be in their presence any longer. Besides, Zander needs to know that some of King Armik's people are defecting. It will be up to him to decide what to do with that knowledge. I wish we knew where this new village is, but something tells me they will not reveal its location. We will be vigilant when hunting in this area in the future though.

"Come, Jodah, let us return."

With a final glance at the two Krijese, we turn back to where I left the dreri. It has been undisturbed, although several shkaba circle the sky above us waiting to pick at the body. Once again, I sling it over my shoulders, and we set off toward our village. The pace is slower going with the burden I carry, but before long, the call of a mellenje reaches us and Jodah returns it. It echoes back and then falls silent.

We stride through the gate guarded by Evren, one of the younger hunters, and Rojtar. They fist their chests as we pass.

"Will you take this to the elders for cleaning?" I ask Jodah. "I want to meet with Zander and let him know of this new development with the Krijese."

"Of course."

I transfer the dreri to him and we part in opposite directions. The village buzzes with activity. Kits run around chasing one another with their laughter ringing through the air. Warriors are moving about, as are females. The central fire is blazing, and a few humans and Tavikhi alike are gathered around it preparing the midday meal.

I pass several tents Zander assigned to the human families that came to stay. They sit outside their dwellings, but don't mingle amongst the tribespeople. I force myself to remember the conversation with my brother. Perhaps as they grow accustomed to us and us to them, they will become more active members of the village. From my understanding, the shefira is working to bridge the distance between the humans and the Tavikhi.

Zander's tent is the largest of the village and sits near the back, closest to the hills that border us. As I suspected, he is not there. Being Shefir, he tends to check on everything to make sure there is nothing the tribespeople need. He also spends time with the elders who tell him stories of our baba.

On my way toward the place where the elders keep all their tents close together, Zander steps out of the healer's hut. I approach and stop before him.

"How did the hunt go today?" he asks as he continues walking. "Did you manage to fell any dhibani?"

I fall in line with him. "No, but we did bring back a dreri big enough to give us food for at least three turns of the sun."

"Excellent."

"We also encountered two Krijese."

His eyes turn stormy and his trail thrashes with vicious swipes. "They should not be this far from their village."

"According to them, King Armik is letting his people starve while keeping all their food stores for himself. They confirmed what his emissary said about them dying out and how few females there are. They, along with a handful more, left to form a separate village full of those who want peace and because their hunting grounds are also depleted."

Zander is silent as we pass various tribespeople. He glances over at me.

"What do you believe?"

"I asked Jodah the same thing, and I agree with him. The two Krijese did not appear well-fed. Their clothes were also tattered and in need of repair. Most telling though is that they were on guard at our approach, but neither drew their weapon in spite of us having ours. No more were in wait to ambush us. They did not act as we would expect Krijese to act."

A small sound rumbles from his chest. "Tomorrow, I want you and another warrior to search out this new village of theirs. If you find it, observe them and their behavior—but don't approach—and discover if what they say is true."

I bring my fist to my chest. "I will report back."

"Ah, there is my *keeshla* and her tribe sisters."

My gaze jerks in the direction he faces, and the five females are walking a short distance away, surrounded by several kits all speaking at once. Laughter lights all their faces and my eyes are drawn to Remi. This is the first I've seen her since yesterday's evening meal. Jodah and I left before the morning meal. She limps, but not as bad as yesterday. Her laughter carries across the distance and is the sweetest sound. She lifts her head and our eyes meet. The smile falls from her lips.

"I don't want a mate."

I walk away and head for my tent.

CHAPTER 8

Seeing Zydon standing there makes something inside me jolt. Especially in the way he looks at me for a split second before turning and walking away. Then another emotion takes its place. Hurt. Although why should I be hurt? I've already decided he'd be the last person I'd choose for a mate. Except that string in my chest is plucked again and releases with a sharp, stinging ping.

"Shefira, tell us again about the Wild West and the animals you call horses," Talek begs. "Could they really run as fast as a dreri and carry a male on their backs?"

London playfully ruffles his long golden hair. "It wasn't just males that rode them. Females did too. And since I've only seen one dreri since I've been here, I can't say exactly, but it definitely appears as though they ran just as fast. Maybe faster."

"I want to ride a dreri," Talek announces and the other kits murmur in agreement. "And wear one of those hats like a cowboy. Although I still do not understand what a cowboy is. You said they do not ride cows—a beast that provides meat, but also a liquid called milk, which is confusing—so why then would they be called a cowboy? Your Earth does not make sense."

I snort, because he isn't wrong. There are so many things about Earth that never made sense to me either. Mostly the fact that not every person is treated equally. It isn't right that someone like me had more opportunities than someone like London, Maeve, or Sage, who I suspect all belonged to the bottom-tier caste. My parents would think that made me better than them. They'd be appalled that these four women are my friends. Well, maybe not Zara. But it's one of the reasons I'm so happy for London. She's essentially the queen here.

We arrive at the central fire and help ourselves to some lunch while the children take off. Once I have my meal, I take a seat on one of the benches. The rest of the girls sit around me.

"How's the warrior that was injured doing?" London asks Sage. "Imir, right? I'm trying to learn all the tribespeople's names."

Sage swallows her food and nods. "He's doing better. Kyler and I think he should be up and about in a few days. He won't be able to return to hunting or fighting right away, but he's healing well."

"That's good news." London turns to Zara. "What about with you and Benham?"

"I'm almost afraid to say in case I jinx it."

"No such thing." I shoulder bump her. "You're doing great. I knew you'd find your thing."

She grins. "You're probably the only one."

"What about you Maeve? I feel like I'm missing out on everything you guys are doing now that I've been relegated to this whole Shefira thing. Something I was wholly unprepared for and that I'm not sure I'm going to be any good at," London admits. "I've always been a follower, not a leader."

"I think you're really good at it," Maeve says in that quiet way of hers, and London smiles down at her. "Alanda is helping me learn the names of all the herbs and vegetables the village grows. There's even this one fruit called a bizele that tastes kind of like this peach I had one time."

I groan. "God, I miss peaches."

"What do they taste like?" Sage asks.

Zara and I exchange glances. "You want to take this one?" She chuckles.

"I'm not sure I can explain it. They're sweet and juicy with almost a flowery—but not—tanginess." I glance down at Maeve. "I want to try one of these fruits you're talking about. Because if they really do taste like a peach, even if it's just a little bit, I will be in heaven."

"Wow," Sage says. "That sounds like high praise. Now I want to try one of them. Do they grow them here in the village?"

Maeve nods. "They're back behind the elders' tents toward the hills."

"I say we go after we're done eating and try one for dessert." I stare at everyone with a big grin and hopeful expression.

Agreements ring out from everyone, and we go back to finishing our meal.

"Hello, *keeshla*." Zander comes up behind London and bends down for a kiss.

Her cheeks darken, but she meets him halfway. It's sweet how he's always touching her and showing affection. When was the last time someone touched me with real affection? I certainly didn't get any from Sinclair and Elizabeth. It most definitely wasn't from the man they were going to force me to marry.

How long did they all stand inside the church with the minister waiting for someone who wasn't going to show up? Did my parents even care, or were they glad to be rid of me? There's a sudden burst of envy in my gut for someone to look at me the way Zander looks at London.

"Hello to you as well, my tribe sisters," Zander greets us next and then turns to me. "Your skills in the training arena have improved greatly in such a short time."

My own cheeks grow hot at the compliment. "Thank you."

"How would you like to go out tomorrow with one of my warriors? It would only be a short scouting trip, but I have confidence in you."

Excitement and nerves flutter in my chest. Am I really ready for that? To leave the safety of the village? The safety of the training arena?

"If you do not feel you are ready—" Zander says as though reading my mind.

"No, no," I rush out. "I am."

He dips his head. "I will let the warrior know you are accompanying him tomorrow then."

"Who will I be going with?" I'm only familiar with a few of the warriors, so I hope it's one of them.

"I will be sending you with Zydon."

What? Oh no. Nope. Not happening. "I don't think that's a good idea."

One of those bony brow ridges lifts. "He is an excellent hunter who is skilled in tracking. You will learn many things under his guidance."

"It has nothing do with his tracking skills." And everything to do with his personality.

"Is there some other reason then that you cannot go with him?" Zander asks with a challenge in his tone.

I blow out an annoyed breath because I haven't been able to back down from a challenge since leaving Earth. I'm not going to let Zydon think I'm scared of being in his presence. "No. Fine. I'll go."

"It is settled." He bends to give London another kiss. "*Keeshla.*"

Once he's gone, I glance around to find the four of them staring at me with expressions ranging from concern—Maeve—to smugness—Zara—and everything in between. London bites her lip and shifts her gaze to her departing husband—her mate. Then she looks back at me with a small wince.

"I'm sorry. I know Zydon probably isn't your favorite person."

I huff. "Like I told Zander, it's fine. It's nothing more than a simple scouting trip. I want to learn everything there is about being a hunter and warrior. I'll take whatever skills Zydon has to teach me so I can get better."

None of them look like they believe me. It annoys me that I had such a strong reaction to a single encounter. He just struck a really sensitive nerve and brought back a lifetime of memories.

"Truly, you guys. I'm willing to forget about it. I may have overreacted. No good comes from holding grudges anyway. We all live together in this village. There shouldn't be any resentment or fighting between our tribespeople. We have enough of that with the Krijese." I slap my thigh. "Now, if you all are done eating, I hear one of those peach-flavored fruits calling my name."

"You and me both," Zara pipes up, and I'm grateful for her help in moving onto another topic.

We all get up, take our bowls back to the fire, and set them in the pile to be washed. I glance over at Maeve.

"You're in the lead. Guide us to these divine fruits please."

She laughs softly. "They're this way."

Like Maeve's the pied piper, we follow her past the tent I share with them and behind the elders' tent. This isn't an area I've explored before. I didn't realize how big the village actually is. Finally, we reach the base of the hill, where there are lines of bushes with oblong purple fruit about the size of a grapefruit growing on them. Maeve stops in front of one and gestures at it. I pluck it off a branch, breathe it in, and glance over at the four of them with excitement.

"Here goes nothing." I don't bother with a tentative bite. Nope, I take the biggest one I can. Juice spills down my chin and drips into my hand that I try to catch it with. I moan in delight, and Maeve laughs. "Oh my god. You guys have to taste this."

London, Sage, and Zara quickly snag one for themselves. More squeals and moans echo mine. London's eyes are wide, and she has a look of pure awe on her face. "I've never had a peach before. This is amazing."

"Never?" I gape.

She shakes her head, and a dark shade of pink rises from the top of her chest to creep up her neck and into her cheeks. "This may not come as a surprise to any of you, but I'm not from the upper tier. Or even the middle one. It was just me and my mom, taking any odd jobs we could find and doing our best to survive. Other than on the rare occasions my mom was able to save up or barter for replicated food, we survived on protein bars. Except, this one time, on my sixteenth birthday, my mom somehow got me the tiniest piece of cake. It was stale, but it was the best thing I ever tasted at the time."

"Oh man, I'm sorry, London," Zara says and squeezes her arm.

London waves her off. "That's all in my past. No one's eating protein bars or replicated meals anymore. We have real food that tastes like peaches."

"That's right." I raise my piece of fruit toward the sky. "Although knowing these are back here is a dangerous thing. I'm probably going to be tempted to sneak a few."

"Alanda says they grow every warm season, so you don't have to worry about them running out," Maeve reassures me.

"That's a relief."

We all take one more piece of bizele and head back toward the main area of the village. We congregate around the central fire and chat a bit more. It's not enough to keep my mind from drifting to thoughts of tomorrow and this scouting trip. What will Zydon say? Will he refuse to let me come along?

I smile distractedly at what I think are the right times, but all I can think about is going out alone with him.

CHAPTER 9

I make my way to the central fire for the morning meal before I have to leave for the hills in search of the Krijese's new location. The sun has barely risen, and my breath is visible in the cold air. I almost struggled to leave the warmth of my tent, but I have a task to complete today. Few people linger around the fire. The rest are staying warm under their furs.

One of the females passes me a bowl of kokrra. I give my thanks and add a small amount of nectar to sweeten it and take a seat on a bench to eat. My gaze wanders, as does my mind. It was a morning similar to this when we last saw Zedam. He set out for hunting and never returned. Still, I have not given up hope that we will find him one day. I blink and my vision focuses. Something in my chest lurches.

Walking toward me is Remi. I cannot take my eyes off her. Her dark hair is woven in a plait that drapes over the front of her shoulder, and her cheeks are the color of manerrat berries. She wears long leg coverings similar to a warrior's and a chest covering with long sleeves. The coverings on her feet are odd and not made of comfortable dreri hide. She carries the wooden staff she is rarely without.

Remi nods in my direction and heads to the fire. I continue to observe her as she has surprised me with the small greeting. After our…disagreement two turns of the sun ago, I did not expect it. Similar to what I did, she adds a generous portion of nectar to her kokrra and, once more to my shock, comes my way. She stops next to me.

"Can I join you?"

I nod. She sits and sets her staff at her feet. I am more than aware that she is close enough for her warmth to cross the distance between us, but not close enough that we touch. My muscles tighten. Do I want Remi to touch me? What happens if my mating marks are not triggered? *What happens if they* are? a louder voice speaks.

She takes a deep breath. "I apologize for snapping at you yesterday. I don't do well with commands. It reminds me too much of Earth, and I left that place for a reason."

I make to deny it had been a command, but I pause. Perhaps it had appeared that way. I am also curious about what her life on her home planet was like. Was it like a prison? "And I apologize for what sounded like a command. It had not been my intention to, as you say, boss you around."

A small smile curls one side of her mouth and my gaze drops to it. Once again, I wonder what it would be like to mouth touch—kiss—with Remi.

"I'm looking forwarding to learning from you today," she says.

I jerk my head back in confusion. "Learning from me?"

She nods. "Zander said I was going with you on some scouting trip today. That you are really good at tracking and such. If I'm going to become a better hunter and warrior, then those are the things I need to learn."

"You are not going with me." The refusal is immediate and abrupt.

Remi recoils. "I'm sorry, what?"

"It is too dangerous. You cannot go."

Her eyes grow stormy and narrow. "I'm pretty sure we just talked about how well I do with commands less than ten seconds ago."

"It is not a simple scouting trip." If it were, perhaps I would not be so concerned for her safety. "Jodah and I encountered two Krijese yesterday while out hunting. They report many of them have left their old village and settled in a new one within the hills where they claim to want to live in peace. *That* is where I am going today. If they lied, then we would be walking into a battle blind. We don't know how many of them reside in this new village."

A flash of fear appears on her face and she stiffens. But then she sits upright. "I don't think your brother would send me if he thought there was any danger."

Zander would never put a female's life at risk, but to suggest that Remi come with me? I do not know what is going through his head. "I will speak to him."

"Speak to him about what?" She turns more toward me, and my gaze drops to how close her leg is to mine. "He's already made his decision and you're not going to try and talk him out of it. I *am* going with you, so you might as well get used to it."

Remi picks up her staff and stands. "I'll finish my breakfast elsewhere and meet you back here in ten minutes. If you try to leave without me, I'll just follow you."

The stubborn female marches in the direction of her tent. By the goddess, I am going to kill my brother when I return. I quickly finish my meal and go back to my own tent for my weapons. I attach my sword to my hip, as well as several daggers. Instead of a spear, I bring my bow and a leather satchel filled with arrows. If I need to, I will be able to take out a few Krijese from a distance before they reach us. I only hope it is not necessary.

With all my weapons, I exit my tent and once again head to the central fire. Remi is already there waiting, her foot tapping an impatient beat.

"Let us go, then, so we can return quickly." I walk past her.

She catches up quickly and we exit through the gate, the two young warriors staring as we pass. I glance at her many times as we move through the small group of fiku trees that stand a short distance away and come out on the other side to the large field. The limp from her injury is barely present, and Remi carries her staff at her side. She scans our surroundings, and it is obvious she is watchful and focused on them.

"What do you see?" I break the tense silence.

She turns her head in my direction and forward again. "I see a large, open field stretching out in front of us and the forest to the left of us. Off to the right are the hills that border the back of the village and run along the length of the field and beyond. There are dhibani on the cliffs of the hills in the distance up ahead."

"And what do you hear?"

Remi's brow with its two furry lines wrinkles. "I hear our footsteps and the grass hitting our bodies. I think I hear at least one bird in the forest. There's also the slight breeze that also rustles the grass."

"And smell?"

Her nostrils flare and she juts her chin out as though that will bring more scents to her. "I smell that same weird, earthy scent that comes from the central fire, which I assume is the wood of the trees. Maybe a faint whiff of some animal shit."

I have heard this word from some of the humans. I am not sure why excrement is a curse, but there are many things about the humans I do not understand. "Very good."

Remi straightens with pride.

"But what about that section of field ahead that has been crushed and trampled? What caused it? Did you also see through the trees there are several dreri standing within the darkness? Can you smell the cold dust that is in the air waiting to fall?" I ask.

She scans for the disturbed field and her eyes dart in the direction of the forest. She raises her head and stares up at the sky. "No, I missed all of those things. We had snow back on Earth, but the leaders of our world devised machines that made everything on the upper tiers sterile. They had ways of pushing all the stench downward to the bottom tier."

The way Remi's voice changes when speaking of Earth tells me it was not a place where she was happy. "I do not know what upper and bottom tiers are."

She glances over as we continue moving through the field and closer to the hills. "You're lucky. They're both awful things. The population of Earth kept growing, so every city—village—kept expanding outward until there was nowhere left to go except up."

This must be what Zander spoke of when he said their dwellings were tall enough to reach the sky.

"Except it's expensive to build up, so only the wealthiest tribe members were able to do so. That left those who didn't have much to stay below," Remi continues. "It also made those people who had money think they were better than those who didn't. It would be like Zander thinking he is better than everyone else in the tribe because he is Shefir."

"He would never think that."

She looks over at me. "No, but where I come from, it's how my people think."

I study her. "And was this upper tier where you dwelled? With the wealthy people who look down on those less fortunate than them?"

"Yes, and I hated it."

Is this the prison she spoke of? "Is that why you came to Tavikh?"

Remi nods. "One of the reasons."

It is hard for me to imagine a place that does not care for all people in the village. How some go without because they do not live in this upper tier. That she hated it speaks of the kind of female she is. I let the silence fall between us and turn my focus back to our surroundings. We are coming close to the spot where Jodah and I spotted the Krijese yesterday.

"Stay alert. Keep your eyes focused on the area near the hills as well as the narrow passages that provide entrance through them."

Remi follows closely at my side with her staff held firmly in her hand. "What are we looking for?"

"Signs of travel. Ground that has been disturbed. Broken limbs or small branches. Flowers that have been crushed. Footprints that do not resemble those belonging to one who wears foot coverings. Anything that appears unusual or out of place." Those are only a few things to keep watch for.

I send up a quick prayer to Deeka to protect Remi from any harm.

CHAPTER 10

Remi

I try to recall all the lessons Rassim taught me during our sparring sessions. My grip on my staff is firm, but not enough to make my fingers stiff, which would make it difficult to wield the weapon if I need to. I do my best to keep watch for all the things that Zydon mentioned. Will I even recognize anything unusual or out of place?

It's not as though I'm familiar enough with this planet yet to know what the *usual* is. Well, aside from the forest filled with black-trunked trees and bright-purple leaves and the yellow grass—bari—that is soft and fluffy, almost waist-high on the Tavikhi and comes in just under my boobs. Thankfully it's been surprisingly easy to move through. I expected it to be like sludge, but it parts with ease as we almost glide through it.

I am also familiar enough with the nenuphar bushes and their blue, flowering buds. As for the hills, they're unlike anything I've ever seen except in old vids. I grew up in the heart of a city surrounded by a city surrounded by another city, and we never ventured out of any of them. We didn't need to. My father's business was there and that's the only thing he cared about. My mother only cared about looking good for his colleagues. The only things I saw ever saw were skyscrapers and more skyscrapers.

What Zydon and the rest of the Tavikhi call hills, I'd call mountains if I were comparing them to the few remaining ones on Earth. Even most of those had been razed to the ground with explosives so more land could be available for buildings. I want to ask Zydon questions, but I'm afraid of making any noise. Except I keep coming back to the fact that Zander would not have sent me out here if he truly thought it was dangerous.

Or maybe this is a test. To see if I'm warrior worthy. If it is, I'm going to prove to both him and Zydon that I am. Which means I need to focus harder on what's around me and ask questions.

"Tell me about the Krijese." I dart a glance to the man— male—at my side. "And why they suddenly want peace. Or at least those that left and came out here."

Zydon hesitates long enough I'm not sure if he'll answer. Is he going to tell me to stop talking? Are we going to spend the rest of our time out here in silence?

"Our tribe has been fighting the Krijese since our baba's baba was Shefir," he finally says. "We were more than happy to live peacefully on this planet with them, but they are a warring tribe. Often even amongst themselves. As time has passed, their numbers have grown smaller. Not only their males, but their females. I do not know if it has been disease or something else. And like us, they have not had any kits born in many seasons."

There's a flash of sympathy for them. It must be terrifying to know that their people are dying out and there is nothing they can do about it. "How awful."

"It is why King Armik's emissary came to see Zander. They have requested a peace treaty between our tribes. Sadly, this does not extend to the humans. They think you are weak, and the Krijese only respect those with power."

I bristle in offense at being called weak. We may lack knowledge and discipline, but strength doesn't always mean in body. "So their people are dying, and no babies are being born. Why, then, would they make their numbers even smaller by leaving?"

"Because, according to them, their king is allowing his people to starve and their hunting lands are no longer plentiful."

I can understand why they wouldn't want to stay in a place like that and don't blame them for leaving. There are more questions I want to ask, but we exit the field onto a clearing where the grass is just over my ankles. The hills are even larger this close. But what I couldn't tell from a distance is that there are plateaus at various heights disguised by trees that grow from the mountain wall. It gives them an almost stair-step-like appearance.

From far away, it looks like one long mountain range. But there are passageways that separate one hill from the next, which allows one hill to overlap the other like a sliding door. I study the path at my feet trying to make out any footprints, but if anyone has passed this way, they were careful to rid their tracks. At least to my untrained eye.

"This way," Zydon directs me quietly.

I follow him as he slips into a crevice in the wall of the mountain. To my surprise, it is actually a pathway that climbs higher upward, with more of the black trees lining either side. As we trek up it, I have to use my staff for leverage. It's steeper than it first appeared. Soon, I'm sweating and struggling to catch my breath. I stare at Zydon's back and how easily he moves, and I refuse to ask him to slow down for me. I've pushed through worse than this.

Except the higher we get, the more difficulty I'm having, and just when I'm finally about to cave, the path levels out and he comes to a stop. I come alongside him, and he turns his head my way and points outward. I look in that direction and can't stop that gasp that escapes.

The sun has slipped out from behind one of the clouds and shines down on the field we'd crossed through, as well as the forest bordering it. The yellow grass flashes and sparkles like molten gold. It's a creamy color that only makes the purple leaves of the trees that much brighter. From up here, there are varying shades from a lilac to a purple-black. And within the branches of several trees are giant nests made from the bari.

Zydon moves to my side and leans in close enough the warmth of his breath caresses my cheek, and the smell of his skin fills my nose—god, is that chocolate?

"Within the nests are mellenje eggs. They should be hatching within the next few turns of the sun. The nene will be returning soon to bring them food. Then she will nestle them until just before the cold season hits."

I turn my head slightly and my gaze drops to lips that are far too close. Zydon's yellow and purple feline eyes meet mine and I nearly stop breathing. A branch snaps somewhere above us, and we both spin toward the sound. I grasp my staff in both hands and the sharp metal sound of him drawing his sword from its sheath echoes around us. Several minutes pass while my heart pounds so hard I can feel it in my ears, but no one appears.

"Come. Let us keep moving," Zydon says, but keeps his weapon in his hand.

Instead of continuing our climb, we descend the trail until we reach the bottom. Just as I reach the opening, he jerks his free hand up near his head. I come to an abrupt stop right before I crash into his back. That's when the sound of footsteps reaches me. He creeps forward slowly, and I step exactly where he does, placing my foot within his footprints to avoid any sticks on the trail.

Two Krijese pass us, but neither glance this way. I shudder in remembrance of the night they attacked the human settlement. I still hear the screams sometimes when I'm lying beneath my furs back at the village. They're speaking to each other about hunting more dhibani and their guttural language—that I'm shocked to be able to under-stand—grates on me. We wait a few beats, and then Zydon ushers me forward. Carefully we step out onto the trail. Up ahead, the Krijese continue walking, seemingly obliv-ious to us trailing them. They turn and disappear within another passageway within the mountains.

I creep closer to Zydon. "Are we going to follow them?"

He nods. "Yes, but we must stay far enough back that they do not sense our presence."

Sounds like a solid plan to me. I'm suddenly rethinking my decision to come as well as Zander's decision to let me. With careful footsteps, I trail Zydon as we slowly climb up the next pathway. This one is different than the last. It's a gradual incline, unlike the other, and the path is wider. There are also tons of clawed footprints as though it's been trekked often.

He stops, and without a word, he steps off the path and into the trees on one side of us. We weave in and out of the dense copse until soft voices reach us. I exchange glances with him, and as we continue forward, I spot a break in the trees up ahead. As we draw closer, the voices grow louder and the scent of meat cooking along with a fire grows stronger.

Zydon stops behind a massively round tree that both of us fit behind without any parts poking out. We each peek around the edge on opposite sides. There, in the clearing, are several tents. Eight, maybe ten. And walking around the small village are Krijese. By my count, there can't be more than fifteen or twenty. Each one is gaunt and definitely doesn't look like they've been eating well. A fire burns in the center, and what appears to be a small dreri is being roasted over it.

There are several elder Krijese seated near to it with hands outstretched for warmth. Their black, ropey, snake-like hair is streaked with gray, and their skin appears faded and dull. From one of the tents a child exits. Judging by his height, I would put him around Talek's age—which I've come to understand is about ten—but he is malnourished so maybe he's actually older. A second one, who is just as skinny—joins him, and the two approach the fire. It's hard to tell from this distance, but they appear to stare long-ingly at the roasting animal that isn't nearly enough to feed all of them.

Despite my fear of the Krijese, my heart aches for the ones in front of us. Anyone can see they're starving. I take a step back, and beneath my foot a branch snaps. Heads whip in our direction, and I flinch. *Shit.* The elder Krijese move toward the children as though to protect them, while the adult Krijese reach for their weapons.

"I mean you no harm," Zydon calls out and before I can guess his intent, he steps out from behind the tree with his sword sheathed and arms raised and walks toward the fire.

Damn him. Indecision wars inside me. Do I charge ahead, or do I wait things out and then run back to the village for backup if I need to? A voice tells me to stop and wait. *Please, Zydon, don't get yourself killed.*

CHAPTER II

Zydon

Protecting Remi is my only thought when I step out from our hiding place. I pray to Deeka she stays out of sight.

"I am not here to fight," I repeat, keeping my hands away from any of my weapons and stopping just outside the central circle they've created.

None of the Krijese relax. Instead, their gazes scan the area behind me as their bodies remain in defensive positions with their weapons drawn. One of their tribespeople steps forward. He is the same one we encountered yesterday.

"Why have you come then, if not to fight? Have you been sent here to count our numbers so you can bring back more warriors and wipe us out for good?" he growls.

"I was sent here to count your numbers, yes, but only to seek the truth of what you spoke. The history between our tribes leaves our shefir hesitant to accept your word without proof." Has Remi left to go seek help, or does she remain where I left her?

"Where is your other warrior?" the Krijese who I suspect is their leader asks. "The one who hunted with you?"

"He remained in our village."

Disbelief is in his narrowed gaze. "Your shefir sent you here alone, when we could have been lying to you? One Tavikhi warrior against an unknown number of Krijese could mean your death if we chose so."

I dip my head. "And yet he trusted that you spoke the truth, which is why I'm here."

After several long tense beats, the Krijese slowly sheath their weapons. Their leader steps a few paces closer but remains at a safe distance for both of us.

"Tell your shefir that we speak the truth." He sweeps his arm out to encompass the whole clearing. "This is all of those who have left King Armik's rule. As you can see, we are few, including elders, females, and two kits. We did not lie."

"That is the only reason I am here. Nothing more," I assure him. "So long as you remain peaceful, we have no quarrel with you."

"Do not return here, Tavikhi. It will be seen as a sign of distrust and aggression if you do. While we came here to live out whatever time we have left, we are not afraid to die." He juts his chin out. "Now, take the female I scent hidden within the trees and leave this place."

Remi. I walk backwards, not taking my eyes off the Krijese until I reach the treeline. It is only then I give him my back and move to where I left her. She remains hidden, and when I come into her sight, she lets out a long sigh and loosens the grip on her weapon.

"Quickly, let us go."

She does not hesitate. I make sure to stay behind her in case we are followed and ambushed, but we make it down the trail and enter the field without incident. It isn't until we are halfway across when Remi finally speaks.

"Holy shit," she says, nearly out of breath, and then stops abruptly. "Don't ever do that to me again."

I halt as well and face her. "Do what?"

She growls and jabs her finger toward the hills. "That. You put yourself in danger trying to protect me. They could have killed you."

"They did not though."

"But they *could have.* And where would that have left me? Up there. Alone," her voice cracks and she storms past me.

"Remi."

"Don't 'Remi' me." She doesn't slow down.

I quickly catch up and, without thinking, grasp her arm. A burning sensation flares through my hand, and suddenly my entire body is on fire. My eyes drop to where I'm touching her and widen at the sight of my mating marks appearing. I lift my head and Remi's gaze follows the same sight up my arm and across my chest—behind which my heart pounds—and then it snaps up to meet mine.

She jerks out of my grip and marches away. "You've got to be kidding me."

Disbelief, awe, and fear have me frozen as I stare at the still darkening mating marks that travel up my arms. I glance down and some are stretched across my sides. There has only ever been a sliver of hope since Zander's mating that perhaps Deeka would bless more males with their mates. However, I would never let the emotion gain strength so as to not be disappointed later.

Forgive me, Deeka, for doubting you.

I stare at Remi's retreating figure. At my *keeshla*. A wave of protectiveness rushes through me. As does pride. Deeka has given me a fierce warrior as a mate. But the words I overheard her speak return to me making my heart sink.

"I don't want a mate."

Such a thing has never existed. Tavikhi females may not have mating marks, but the bond is triggered in them at the same time as their mate. They both feel it, and it only grows stronger with each turn of the sun. Except it is clear humans do not feel the same bond as a Tavikhi. London did not, and it would appear Remi does not either.

I move quickly to catch up with her as she reaches the edge of the forest. She only briefly glances in my direction, her gaze traveling over my mating marks, before she keeps her gaze trained ahead.

"Are we going to speak about this?" I would like to talk before we reach the village where everyone will be offering words of joy. And before my brother sees my marks.

"I don't particularly want to, no."

"Is being my mate truly that awful?"

Remi stops walking and turns to face me. She lets out a ragged sigh. "It is if I'm mated to someone who won't let me be me. Or who doesn't think of what I might care about. Who tries to tell me what I can and can't do as though I am nothing more than a child."

I recoil. "I do not think of you as a child."

She raises both furry lines above her eyes. "Oh really? Wasn't it you who, only hours ago, tried to forbid me from coming with you today? Or what about the other day, when you demanded I go to the healer? You didn't even bother to ask me if I was okay. You just assumed I wasn't capable of making my own decision to see Sage or Kyler."

"I did not do any of those things because I think you incapable." From all I have witnessed, Remi is intelligent, strong, and fierce.

Remi clenches her staff tightly. "Well that's how it felt. My parents made me feel that way too. Always telling me what or what not to do. They didn't let me make any of my own decisions, even if they might have been shitty ones."

Shame fills me that I have made her feel this way. "Is this the prison you spoke of to the other female?"

She jerks her head up and narrows her eyes. "What, are you spying on me now?"

"I overheard you speaking with your tribe sister when I passed your tent on the way to my own. It was not my intention to intrude on your privacy." I cross my fist over my chest. "On my honor."

Remi finally relaxes. "I'm sorry for accusing you."

Carefully I reach for her hand. She jerks but does not pull away. There is a slight tingle where we touch, and my mating marks flare bright again before turning a shade darker. Her skin is both soft and rough beneath mine. I study the callouses that have formed on her palm from sparring and trace a line from one to the next. Remi trembles and I lift my head to meet her eyes. Her skin color changes along her cheeks.

My gaze drops to her lips and her tiny tongue darts out to wet them. I step closer until she tips her head back to remain looking at me. Unable to resist, I lower my head and lightly press my mouth to hers as I have seen Zander do to London. A pleasant sensation runs through me. I can understand what there is to like about kissing. There is a connection between two mates that brings them closer to each other than anyone.

I straighten and stare down at my beautiful mate. The color on Remi's face has darkened. Perhaps that is similar to what my mating marks do.

"That was very pleasurable." I cannot wait to do it again.

She laughs and it is the most wonderful sound. "It was nice."

I will take nice. For the moment. "Come, let us return to the village and report our news of the Krijese village to Zander."

Remi hesitates briefly and then gives a small nod. Although I would like to keep touching her, I release the hand I'm still holding, and we enter the forest. One of these days, I will take her up into the trees and show her the beauty to be found up there.

I remain on guard during our trek and only relax at the call of the mellenje. We stride through the clearing and the small copse of trees before coming out a short distance from the gate. The two warriors at the entrance gape at me and their gaze shifts to Remi. A flash of envy crosses both their faces. I send up a prayer to Deeka that more of our males are as lucky as Zander and me and find their mates.

We continue across the village and more eyes track us. Whispered voices reach my ears. My mate takes a step closer to me and leans in.

"How long are they going to stare at us?" she says in a low voice.

"Perhaps for one or two turns of the sun. Deeka has now blessed another warrior with a mate after far too long. It is a cause for celebration. We represent hope to the others. If she has blessed two of us with mates, what else might she bless us with?"

Remi nods slowly. "I guess I didn't think of it that way."

The closer we get to the central fire, the more tribespeople have gathered. I straighten with pride. Word must have spread fast, because Zander and his *keeshla* are hurrying our way.

CHAPTER 12

What the heck am I going to do? I quickly glance at Zydon and his mating marks before London and Zander overtake us. He thinks we're mates because of those tattoos and some blessing by the goddess, and I'm not sure I even like him. Or that he likes me. Despite that brief but powerful kiss.

"I knew it," London says with far too much satisfaction before throwing her arms around me. "I just knew you two were mates."

"Congratulations, brother," Zander says and clasps forearms with Zydon. "Deeka has blessed you with a fine mate."

The male in question's eyes meet mine and a light shines from within them. "Yes, she has."

I hate to burst everyone's bubble, but I'm not sure I'm ready to accept the fact. We've argued more times than not. Just because Zydon appears to have so easily accepted it, doesn't mean I have to. I'm not entirely opposed to the idea of a mate—at least up until now—but I need time to think things through.

"If you'll excuse me, I'm going to get some water from the river to heat and wash up." I jerk my chin toward Zander, but I speak to Zydon. "You should probably tell your brother what you found."

Without waiting for anyone's response, I take off toward my tent to grab a bowl to bring back water in.

"I hope you don't think you're going to get away from me that easily, Remi Alcott," London calls out from behind me.

Blowing out a breath, I slow my pace so she can catch up. I might as well get this conversation out of the way. She reaches me, wraps her hand around my arm, and keeps walking.

"Don't gloat. Please."

"I won't, I promise," she says. "Do you want to tell me what happened out there though?"

"We found the Krijese camp. It's exactly as they say. There were only a couple handfuls of them, and it was clear they're starving. The two children that I saw were so scrawny. Nothing like the Tavikhi children. As much as they scare the shit out of me, I feel sorry for them. At least the ones up in the mountains who I do believe want peace." We near my tent.

"That's fine and all, but I want to hear about you and Zydon."

Since washing up was merely an excuse to get away, I gesture her inside. I grab the torch and bring it in with me to plant in the ground near our fire pit. She settles cross-legged on Zara's pallet near mine, and I sit as well. I pluck at the callouses on my palm and can still feel Zydon running his finger along them.

"Like I said yesterday, I wasn't holding any grudges and wanted to learn from him. So, I showed up at the central fire for breakfast and sat with him. Said I was looking forward to today. The first words out of his mouth were that I wasn't going."

London winces. I toss up my hand. "Exactly. I told him I was going anyway and to get over it. After that, things got better, thankfully. We had a real conversation. He pointed out different animal tracks and ways to spot if someone had been through the area or not. It was all going great."

"Until?"

I huff. "Until we came across the Krijese camp. We'd been hiding within the forest observing them, and I stepped on a branch alerting them to our presence. They all drew their weapons, and without giving me any warning, Zydon steps out with his sword still sheathed. He just walked out there knowing they could have killed him."

London sits quietly for a minute before she scoots next to me and takes my hand. "Did you ever think that maybe he did it to protect you? To distract them by taking the attention off of you so you could get away and be safe?"

"Of course I did. But it's clear he doesn't know me well if he actually thought I would just run away and leave him there to die." I've never had friends. Only ones who liked me for what I—or my parents, rather—could do for them. Not until that long flight here. That's meant everything to me, so nothing could make me turn my back on them. That includes everyone here in the village.

She murmurs a noise. "Was this before or after his mating marks were triggered?"

"Before." Although I'm not sure what that has to do with anything. "Once they told him to leave, we hurried back down the mountain. I was so mad that I walked away before I said anything I'd regret. He clasped my arm to stop me, and that's when it happened."

"How did he react?" London asks.

"We argued, of course, about how he's treated me during every single one of our few interactions." I pause. As much as I don't want to talk about what happened next, London is the one person I've been the closest to. "He apologized, sort of, and then…he kissed me."

She squeals and bounces up and down, but I hold up my hand. "It barely even qualified as a kiss."

"Probably because Tavikhi don't know what kissing is. Zander had no idea. He kept calling it mouth touching." She giggles.

Well for someone who's never done it before, Zydon did a pretty good job. "I don't know that I want a mate," I confess. "We don't even know each other."

"Babe, we've only been in the village a week." London squeezes my hand. "Of course you don't. That doesn't mean you can't get to know each other. From what Zander has said, his brother—all the males, really—have resigned themselves to being alone and without a mate for the rest of their lives. They believe wholeheartedly in their goddess and all her blessings. Which means that, for Zydon, even if you've had disagreements, you're his mate. For better or worse."

"It's the worse I'm worried about."

London glares. "Where's the Remi I met on the ship? The one who was ready to tackle anything, because she wasn't going to let anything hold her back? The one who is confident in herself and who told me not that long ago that she wants to experience everything our new home has to offer?"

I narrow my eyes. "You know, it's not very nice to throw my words back in my face."

"Get over it." She sticks her tongue out at me. "*This* is our life. These *people* are our lives. And look, I'm not saying you have to agree to the whole mate thing, but I want you to give it a chance. It's kind of incredible if you think about it."

I snort. "You're just saying that because you're getting alien dick."

"Oh my god." London pushes me over and I laugh. "I expect something like that to come out of Zara's mouth, not yours."

"What do you expect to come out of my mouth?" The woman in question steps into the tent. "And what has Benham bitching 'by Deeka's flame, not another one'?'"

London and I share a glance and I sigh. It's not as though it's going to stay a secret for long. "Zydon's mating marks were triggered today."

Zara's eyes widen. "By who?"

I stare at her expectantly and she nearly falls over laughing. "You? Oh shit. This Deeka lady has a damn sense of humor."

"Just wait until you're someone's mate, and we'll see who's laughing then," I harrumph.

She shrugs. "I'm game for it. A ripped alien hottie with a tail that probably does some wicked naughty things and absolutely adores me? Where do I sign up?"

My cheeks heat, and even in the firelight, I can tell London's face changes color. *Their tails?* Great, now I have something else to invade my dreams.

London claps her hands. "All right, enough hiding. We're all going to go out to the central fire and eat our midday meal. Remi, you're going to let people *ooh* and *aah* over this blessing, because it means a lot to them. And Zara, you're not going to mention naughty and wicked tails to anyone else."

"Man," Zara groans. "You were a lot less bossy before this Shefira thing."

I nod in agreement.

"Yeah, well, if that's who I'm supposed to be now, then I need someone to practice on. And you two"—London points at us both—"get to be my guinea pigs."

Zara and I exchange glances and snicker.

"Yay, lucky us," she deadpans.

London groans and stands. "C'mon, you two."

I take her outstretched hand, as does Zara, and she helps us to our feet. Zara grabs the torch and leads the way. London lays her hand on my arm. I glance at her.

"Everything is going to work out," she says with far more confidence than I'm feeling. "You'll see."

The sunlight and the bitter cold hit me the second I step outside. Still holding on to me, London and I walk while Zara strides forward with the fearlessness and bold self-assurance she's perfected to hide all her insecurities. I envy her, because as much as I try, I don't do it nearly as well.

We pass tribespeople moving about the village and most of them don't pay us any more attention than their bowed heads in respect for their shefira. But the ones who stare and whisper to each other make me self-conscious. Not many people sit around the fire. Probably because of the falling temperature.

Zara grabs three bowls, passes two over, and once we all help ourselves to the food, we take our usual seats on the giant log that's been crafted into a backless bench. Sage and Maeve should be here soon. It's been our ritual to make sure we all have lunch together to talk about our day and anything going on. Mostly because it's the time of day when most of the tribespeople are either out patrolling, hunting, or going about their tasks around the village.

I take a bite and happen to see over London's shoulder. Both Zander and Zydon are coming toward us, their mating marks glaringly obvious against the lighter purple skin. Except it's the man—male—on the left I can't take my eyes off.

CHAPTER 13

I am impatient to go find my mate. Remi's going to wash up was a ploy to get away. From me or from the need to avoid the stares and whispers I do not know. But reporting our findings to Zander is important. As is discussing his reasoning for putting my mate in possible danger.

"She could have been captured or killed." My tail thrashes.

"I trust you and Jodah completely. If you both felt the Krijese spoke the truth about wanting peace, then I trusted your judgment. I would not have put my *keeshla's* tribe sister in danger if I had any idea that the males you came across had been lying."

That doesn't soothe my anger. "What if we were all wrong? What if they killed me? We both know the Krijese under King Armik's rule have tried to breed with the humans. Remi would have been defenseless against them."

"Your mate is far from defenseless. She is not the first female to become a warrior, even if the others are no longer with us," Zander points out. "Would you have this same response if it had been one of them with you? Would they, too, have been defenseless?"

He already knows the answer to these questions.

"No, they would not have," he answers for me. "If you are going to get Remi to accept this mate bond and fall in love with you, then you need to understand how important becoming a warrior is to her."

I do not like that my brother knows more about my mate than I do. *Perhaps you should get to know her then.* "How did you get London to accept it?"

"With patience and listening to what she wanted and what made her happy. There is no feeling greater in the world than to see your mate's joy."

It would appear that I am going to have to learn how to control my impulsiveness. Perhaps the second part will come easier. I have already discovered at least one thing that makes Remi happy.

"I will think on what you say."

Zander claps my shoulder. "Come, let us go find our mates. Word has already begun to spread through the village that your mating marks were triggered."

We exit his tent and make our way to the central fire. Tribespeople lay their fists over their chests as we pass. Even the humans have come outside to observe. Their gazes linger on my brother's and my mating marks, but their emotions are difficult to read, which is unusual. More often fear and caution are written on their faces. Are they happy as our other tribespeople are?

There, seated beside the shefira and the female with hair color similar to ours, is Remi. Something inside me shifts. She lifts her gaze as though sensing my presence and it meets mine. My chest swells. This is the female Deeka sent to me. After all these seasons.

I head straight for her. It is time for me to learn more about my mate. The shefira stands and greets Zander with a kiss. He wraps his arm around her and his tail twines around her leg. The one with hair a similar color to ours coughs and rises.

"As much fun as this is going to be, I'll let you all have some privacy," she says and leaves.

"Hello again," I greet Remi.

Her smile is not the full one I have seen her give her tribe sisters. I gesture to the empty place beside her.

"May I take my meal with you?"

She cocks her head and narrows her eyes. "Why are you being weird?"

London coughs as well. Are the females getting sick? But then I return to her question. "I do not understand."

"You're being all polite and formal. It's weird."

Does she want me to be rude?

"We'll leave you two to talk," the shefira says and she nudges Zander, who bows his head and guides her away from the fire.

Even though Remi has not answered, I sit beside her. It brings back the memory of the morning meal when we sat on a nearby bench. Had it only been this morning that I wondered what would happen if we touched?

"Did you tell Zander about what we found?" she breaks the silence, and I blink away the image.

"Yes."

Her eyes widen and she gestures with her hand. "And? What did he say?"

"We will leave them in peace as they have asked. The hunting lands here are plentiful and there is more than enough that no one will go hungry."

Remi nods. "That's good. I'm still not a fan of them, but I did feel bad for the two children. They looked starved."

My mate has a gentle heart and kindness in her soul for those less fortunate. "The only concern Zander has is that King Armik will not take kindly to his people leaving. It can be seen as a betrayal to him."

"What happens if he causes problems for them? Are we going to offer them protection like you did the human settlement or let them fend for themselves?" Remi asks.

These are good questions I do not have answers for. "That will be up to our shefir."

"I'm pretty sure London might have a few words to say about it as well."

"We will keep an eye on them without encroaching on their new village. Perhaps there is no need for concern." Although I'm not sure I believe that. From my mate's expression, I'm not sure she does either.

"Mmhmm."

Rassim approaches with his staff in hand and takes in my mating marks. His gaze turns to Remi and a smile plays on his lips.

"Many blessings on your mating." He fists his chest as he comes to a stop in front of us.

"Thanks," my mate says in a tone that does not match her word.

"Are you ready for our sparring session?"

Remi rises. "Always. Are you ready to get spanked again?"

Surely my translator is malfunctioning. My mate is not hitting Rassim on his tail side, is she? "She is not going to spar with you."

My mate whirls on me with fire in her eyes. "You are unbelievable. Just because you have those stupid marks on you doesn't mean I'm going to let you boss me around anymore than I was going to without them."

Her words about my marks sting, but I hold up my hands. "Peace, *keeshla*. Again, it was not my intent to boss you around. I merely mean that you won't be sparring with Rassim, because you will be sparring with me."

Some of the anger drains from her. "You? You're going to spar with me?"

"If you are agreeable to it."

Remi glances at Rassim and then back at me. "You're not going to go soft on me are you? Just because of those marks? Because if you are, then no, I'm not agreeable. Rassim and the other few warriors I've sparred with know they better not hold back. I deserve to be treated as just another opponent."

It goes against how I believe my mate should be treated, but if I want her to accept this mate bond, then I must do as Zander says and find out what makes my mate happy. "On my honor, I will teach you what I know and not—as you say—go soft on you."

She stares down at me, and I stare back, hoping she sees that I am sincere in my offer. Finally, she nods. "Okay then. Let me go get my staff."

Rassim steps back as she rushes over to the fire and places her bowl with the others and then takes off in the direction of her tent. He turns to me.

"She is a fine mate."

If he were not already mated to Alanda, I would not appreciate his words. But as I know they are bonded in the true sense, I let the flare of jealousy that rises die down. "Yes, she is."

"Teach her as you would any of the young warriors or the kits. Also know that, just as they would, she could be slightly injured. Trust her to know when she has had enough." With that advice, Rassim walks away and heads toward the hill that leads down into the arena.

Even from here, the sound of other warriors practicing reaches me. I turn to where Remi went, and already she is returning with her weapon in hand.

"I'm ready," she announces.

"Apologies, *keeshla*. Let me go and get my own weapon and I will meet you in the arena."

Remi tilts her head. "You're not going to bail on me, are you?"

"Bail on you?"

"You know. Conveniently forget that you said you were coming back and find something else to do while I wait for you."

It is then I notice the rigid way she holds herself. As though she expects me to do that very thing. I take the few steps that separate us, and she looks up at me. I like that Remi is taller than the other human females, but still small to me. I lay my hand on her cheek, and she does not flinch away. Instead, it feels as though she leans into my touch. Her skin is so different than mine. Softer. Smoother. I could spend many turns of the sun just touching her like this.

"Has someone done this to you in the past? Bail on you?"

She exhales a harsh laugh. "Yeah, you could say that."

"Who did this to you?" I am angry at whoever put this look of sorrow in my *keeshla's* eyes.

"My parents. People who pretended to be my friend." She is looking anywhere but at me, and her face turns color again.

It would appear I will have to work hard to earn my mate's trust. "*Keeshla*, Remi, on my honor, I will never bail on you for anything. If I make a promise to you, I will keep it."

At last, she lifts her gaze to mine and studies me. To my surprise, she lays her hand over mine and rises up to kiss me softly on the lips. It is, once again, only a brief caress, but that she is the one to initiate it gives me hope.

"Thank you," she says. "Now, are *you* ready to get spanked?"

"Why would I be ready for you to hit my tail side?"

Her beautiful laughter fills my ears, and she wraps her hand around my arm and tugs me forward. "Come on. I'll explain what it means to get spanked on our way to get your staff."

CHAPTER 14

REMI

My cheeks have to be flaming red. I can't believe I kissed Zydon. Not that it was much of a kiss, but still, I made the first move. I want to do it again. And more. *Slow down, you. Let's not get ahead of ourselves here. There's still the whole not being sure about this mate business.*

True, but it doesn't mean we can't try the kissing thing again. Does it?

"Remi," Zydon's voice brings me back. "You were going to explain this spanking to me."

Ah, yeah, right. His confusion is kind of adorable really. "It just means that I'm going to win."

Those bone ridges where his eyebrows should be shift. "Then why do you not just ask if your opponent is ready to lose?"

I snort. "Because it doesn't have quite the same ring to it. Telling someone they're going to get spanked is called trash talking. It's a way to make your opponent lose their confidence."

"Your human language is very confusing." Zydon shakes his head.

"Oh, I totally agree. We have words that are spelled the same way but are pronounced entirely differently. A single word can have three different meanings. It's ridiculous really."

We reach his tent, and he opens the flap. "Would you like to come in?"

Other than the night we arrived in the village and slept in the storage tent, I've never seen the inside of anyone else's except the one I share with the other girls. I'm a little curious what his looks like. I set my staff against the outer hide and step past him. It's hard to judge in the dim light given off by the small fire that burns in the center pit, but Zydon's home might be slightly bigger than mine. It also smells like a combination of the pungent yet fruity scent the fire gives off and some type of floral fragrance. There's also a faint hint of the chocolate-like way he smells. I like it. A lot.

On one side of the fire is a large pallet of furs. I quickly glance away and turn to one of several wooden chests that line one wall. Nearby is his wooden staff, propped against the wall. My gaze darts to Zydon who is watching me examine his dwelling with an indecipherable expression. His mating marks are even darker against his lighter purple coloring, and I have an impulsive urge to run my fingers over them. Is his leather-looking skin as buttery-soft as London says it is? What appeared to be a large tent before suddenly feels a whole lot smaller.

"Your place is lovely."

He bows his head. "I am pleased you like it."

We both stand there awkwardly—or at least I do—until I finally clear my throat. "Um, we should probably get down to the arena if we're going to spar."

"Of course." Zydon crosses the space and grabs the staff.

I rush outside and take in a deep breath, hoping to cleanse the far too enticing scent that clung to the interior of his tent. He steps out behind me and gestures in the direction of the arena. I grab my weapon and move at a clip. It doesn't take long before Zydon catches up.

"If you are interested, I would be happy to show you how to use a sword and daggers as well," he breaks the silence.

I whip my head to the side, shocked at his offer. "You would?"

He nods. "If you truly wish to become a hunter and warrior, then you will need to learn to defend yourself with more than your stick. From what I have seen, you wield it well, but if you are going to bring down a dhibani or dreri, then you will need more than that."

Unable to stop myself, I throw my arms around him and squeeze tight. "Thank you."

"You are welcome."

I loosen my hold, a bit too conscious about how good Zydon smells and feels, and we continue walking until we're down the slope and on level land. I take my place within the dirt-packed arena and tie up my hair. He stands opposite me until I finish, and we both move into a defensive pose. He strikes first. We trade blows, the sound of wood crashing together echoing around us. His fighting style is different than Rassim's, and I try to adjust.

Zydon aims for my side with a sharp jab. I spin, dodging out of the way, but he anticipates my move, because his weapon hits my ass. I whirl on him, and he's grinning.

"Perhaps it is I who will *spank* you," he says far too arrogantly and with a hint of suggestion in his tone that makes me think he means more than winning our sparring session.

Now I'm imagining us in his tent with me draped over his lap with my butt bared and raised in preparation. I'm so focused on that, I almost miss Zydon's next blow. I manage to block it, but the ricochet vibrates down the length of my weapon and jars my hands so much I nearly lose my hold. I curse and quickly tighten my grip.

"You are distracted, *keeshla*."

My chest heaves with effort and sweat dampens my forehead. It's hard enough to breathe, so I keep my mouth shut and go on the offensive. I push Zydon back. Left strike. Right. There's a tiny opening at his chest and I jab the end of my staff toward it, but at the last minute, he jerks his stick upward and deflects my blow. In the same move, he swings it downward in an arc at my feet and catches me before I can jump.

I fall and land on my back, pushing all the air out of my lungs with a groan. *Damn it.* I smack the ground next to me with an open palm, and a cloud of dust explodes. A shadow falls over me and Zydon comes into view. I take his outstretched hand and he heaves me up to my feet but doesn't release me. Instead he pulls me close and leans down with his lips far too close to mine.

"I think I enjoy this spanking you speak of," he whispers against them.

My nipples tighten as the timbre of his voice washes over me, and a warm heat settles low inside my belly. "Don't get used to it."

I hook my leg behind his and push. Except I make a tactical error. I forget Zydon's hold on me. He tumbles to the ground but takes me with him. I land on top of him. Chest to chest. Pelvis to pelvis. I stare down at him, and his near-black vertical pupils dilate. My gaze drops to his lips and I'm just now noticing how thick they are. Remembering how soft they felt against mine.

There's the sensation of something gliding high along the back of my legs and twining around them. His tail? Zander is always wrapping his around London when she's close to him. She says it's because he always wants to be touching her in some way.

"Perhaps we both got spanked." Zydon smirks.

I find myself answering with a grin of my own. "Maybe we did."

A shadow falls over the both of us and I crane my neck. Zander stands there with an amused look.

"I see neither of you has killed the other," he snarks.

Quickly, I push myself off Zydon and clamber to my feet while he rises a bit slower. Once again, the sensation of his tail circling around my waist sends sparks dancing across my skin.

"All is well, brother?" Zydon asks.

Zander dips his head. "I was tasked by my *keeshla* to check on her tribe sister and see that she is well. But I can see there is nothing for London to worry about."

"Nothing at all," Zydon answers since I've apparently gone mute.

My cheeks heat at the way Zander's gaze lingers over the both of us and drops to where Zydon's tail firmly grips my waist before returning to our faces. I dart a quick glance to my left and several warriors linger nearby staring at the three of us. While I'm a bit self-conscious about the attention, I don't want to draw any more by making a big deal out of it.

Is that the excuse you're telling yourself?

Fine, maybe I like the way his tail feels around me.

"I shall let her know." Zander casts one more glance at Zydon's tail before he makes his way up the hill and disappears from view.

"You can let me go now." I turn my head to Zydon.

"I am not sure I want to. I enjoy holding my mate close." He leans down. "I think you enjoy it as well."

"Whether I do or don't isn't the point. We can't just keep standing here," I point out. "We either need to spar again or we part ways. You go off and do whatever it is you do, and I'll head back to my tent."

"Perhaps I do not want to part ways, but I also do not want to spar."

I stare up at Zydon and I like the fact that, while he's taller than me, he's not so tall I get a cramp looking at him. Why am I suddenly breathless? "What is it you want to do then?"

"I would like to try more of this kissing. It is extremely pleasurable." His gaze drops to my mouth. "But I do not want company for it. I would like to spend time with you. Alone. Kissing. And getting to know my mate."

Man, I really should be putting the brakes on this mate business, but this Zydon I'm seeing now is someone I also would like to get to know better. Not the imperious one. But this one that is sweet, a little flirty, and who actually has a sense of humor. I like this side of him. Maybe a bit too much. Because what if it's just a ploy? He's nice until he gets whatever it is he wants from me and then I'm not of any use to him.

A warm hand cups my jaw and I blink.

"What put that faraway look in your eyes, *keeshla*?"

I paste on a fake smile. The one I used around my parents and their sycophants. "Sorry, I actually told Zara I'd meet up with her after I sparred this afternoon."

"You did not answer my question, Remi."

Maybe if Zydon's tone had been more demanding I could have blown him off or made some other excuse. But it wasn't. It was soft, pleading almost.

God, I'm so tired of letting my past insecurities rule me. I take his hand and tip my head. "Come on. We should probably talk."

He untwines his tail from me and lets me lead him away from the arena and in the direction of his tent.

CHAPTER 15

I do not like the faraway look that entered Remi's eyes. It was as though she had gone somewhere else. And not to a good place either. I gently squeeze her hand for encouragement. I want my mate to be able to speak to me about whatever troubles her as I would speak mine to her.

To my surprise, she leads me not to her tent, but mine. Remi paces back and forth with her arms wrapped around her waist. I snag her hand and she stops.

"Let us sit," I suggest.

She nods, but there is a hesitancy to it. I lower myself to my furs and wait patiently for her to join me. My instinct tells me not to push, but rather let her make the decision of what she would like to do next. Finally, Remi sits at the other end of my sleeping place. I would have liked for her to have chosen to be closer, but I also sense she needs the space as a form of protection. Not for her body, but her heart.

I have never been good at waiting. Zander and Zedam were always the most patient of the three of us. But for my *keeshla* I will wait for as long as I need until she is ready to unburden herself to me. Many beats of my heart later, that patience is, at last, rewarded.

Remi clears her throat and picks at the inside of her hand before she lifts her gaze to me. "I already told you a little about my parents and my life back on Earth. About being part of the upper-tier caste. Most people would probably call me crazy for how much I hated it. But it was truly awful."

I want to reach for her hand, but I do not think she's ready for that yet. This is not the bold Remi who told Zander she was going to train with his warriors. This female is hesitant. Cautious. Perhaps fearful as well.

"When you live in the upper tier, everybody wants what you have," she continues. "And they'll do whatever they can to get it. They will pretend to be someone to your face, only the minute you turn around, they stab you in the back."

Remi must see the horror on my face because she laughs quietly. It does not sound the same as her usual one, and I decide I do not like it much.

"I don't mean they literally stab you," she clarifies. "It's just a figure of speech. It basically means they betray you or take advantage of you."

"And you have had many of these people…stab you in the back?" I am coming to hate this planet my mate came from.

"More than I like to think about. It's worse though when it's your parents."

I try to imagine Baba or Nene betraying my brothers or me in any way, but it is not possible. True betrayal is not something we have ever experienced. Not by our own people at least. I no longer can resist touching her to offer whatever comfort she might take from me. I move closer until our legs are touching and my tail can wrap around her waist. She lets me take her hands in mine. They are so small and pale, but also strong.

"How often did they betray you?" Even once is too many.

"So often, I came to expect it. Braced myself for it. As much as I wish otherwise, things like that tend to leave their mark on a person."

"And this is why you think people will bail on you?"

Remi raises and lifts her shoulders in a gesture I have often witnessed the humans do. "Pretty much."

"*I* did not bail you. Yet when I spoke of kissing and spending time alone with you so I may get to know you, you made an excuse to not do so." I try to keep the hurt out of my voice, but I am not sure I succeed. "I know humans do not feel the mate bond like Tavikhi do and that we must earn your affection. That is something I would very much like to do."

"Why?" Remi asks.

That gives me pause. "I do not understand the question."

"Why do you want to earn my affection?"

Because you are my mate, I want to tell her, but there is something more to what she is asking that I cannot figure out. I do not want to say the wrong thing and make things worse. There is only now an uneasy peace between us. Remi must sense my continued confusion because she continues.

"I know you and the other unmated warriors thought you'd be alone for the rest of your lives. And now you have those mating marks just because you touched me. They didn't make either one of us different people than the ones we were before they showed up. We've argued more times than not. Yet suddenly you're ready to kiss and make up like none of that ever happened." Remi breathes in deeply and releases it. "It just feels like some kind of trick."

There is so much hurt and distrust in this mate of mine. From what she has said about her life back on Earth, it is no wonder. Those who are supposed to care the most about her have not shown her any affection. They have made her think someone is kind to her because they must want something.

"My baba and nene were not friends when his mating marks were triggered. In fact, Nene went out of her way to avoid him whenever possible. He was soon to be Shefir of the tribe, and she thought him to be too 'imperious' I believe you would say. They argued frequently." I smile gently. "Perhaps that is why Deeka chose her as his fated mate. So she could teach him how to be less arrogant. Less demanding. Kinder. Gentler. Even after their mate bond was triggered, they still had disagreements. Neither of them changed overnight either."

I lay my hand on the back of Remi's neck and rest my forehead against hers. "Just because I wear these marks does not mean that everything will be perfect between us. But perhaps, with time, you will teach *me* to be less imperious and I will teach you that mates can disagree and argue, but still care for each other without expecting anything in return."

"It just feels too good to be true, you know?" She leans into me. "That I don't have to assume someone always wants something from me. It's all I've ever known."

"You asked me why I want to earn your affection," I remind her. "Because you are strong, fierce, and have a gentle heart. You are loyal to those you love. Any warrior would be blessed with you as a mate. And yet, of all the warriors, Deeka chose me as being worthy of belonging to you. You are a blessing and I want to show her, and most especially, you, that I am deserving of being chosen."

Slowly, I tip my head and fuse my mouth to Remi's. The kiss is as simple as the others, but a pull tells me there is more if only I am patient enough to discover it. There is a flicker against my lips and instinct has me parting them. Her tongue slips inside and brushes up against mine.

So there is more to this kissing than merely mouth touching.

As I do not know what I am doing, I let my mate lead. I will let her teach me all she knows about kissing as I will teach her about hunting and fighting. Her touches to the inside of my mouth are light. Tentative. As though she is testing both of our responses. They only inflame me. My mating marks burn and tingle and my flesh feels too tight. So do my leg coverings. My cock is hard and the nodes that run the length of it throb and fill with mating fluid.

Remi's hand falls to the back of my neck. She grips it hard as she rises up onto her knees, her mouth never leaving mine. She deepens the kiss and grows bolder. I follow her lead and slick my tongue across hers. She tastes of the sweet nectar she uses to sweeten her kokrra. It has always been a favorite flavor of mine, but even more so after receiving Remi's kisses.

Far too soon, the kiss ends. She draws back and I release my light hold on her. To my surprise, she doesn't move far away. Instead, she slowly lies on her back and stares up at me with her cheeks darkening in that color I have discovered can mean anger or shyness. The only heat that flickers in her eyes is desire, so it must mean she is feeling shy.

"I'm not ready for anything more today, but I thought maybe we could try practicing kissing like this," Remi says and reaches for me.

Once again, I let her guide me. I lay on my side—pressing myself against her—and she wraps her arms around my shoulders and tugs me close. Her chest mounds press hard against me with their stiff tips. I want to explore them, but until she offers them to me, I will not. Her hair has come loose and spreads out around her.

"I like this practicing very much." I grin.

Remi returns my smile and releases the laughter I love to hear from her. "Me too. Although you're kind of far away. Maybe you should come closer."

"As you command." I lean down and brush my mouth across hers. As I learned from her, I flick my tongue and she parts her lips, letting me in.

The kiss deepens and I tilt my head to bring us even closer. My cock begs for release, but I ignore it. Instead I focus on my mate and our kisses. Our tongues play, and I study what brings the most reaction from her. What makes her breathing increase. Her small, blunt claws dig into my flesh. I want to bring my mate as much pleasure as she brings me. Not only through touch, but the trust she has offered me. I shall keep it within my heart and hold onto it tightly doing whatever I can to not break it.

CHAPTER 16

Lying here with Zydon while the rest of the village go about their day should bring with it guilt, but I can't manage to feel it. He kissed me until we both grew breathless, and I'd been seconds away from begging him to touch me…everywhere. One of us kept their senses, which, in the end, is probably a good thing. Except I'm struggling to come up with why that is? If I'm giving this mate thing a chance, what's wrong with taking things further?

I'm not sure when I decided to try to make it work. Maybe after the tenth or twentieth kiss in which Zydon demonstrated what a fast learner he is? Or maybe it was after he said he wanted to prove himself deserving of me. No one has ever thought me worthy before. Not my parents. Not the so-called friends I didn't actually have. I've always been the one trying to prove myself to undeserving people.

Except instead of worrying about it, I'm going to enjoy this moment. I cuddle closer to him and breathe in the chocolatey goodness of his skin. He brings the furs up higher, so I'm covered from toes to chin. My fingers play along the mating marks that decorate his naked chest, and his arms tighten their hold on me. It's nice. Far more than nice if I'm being honest with myself.

"How are you not cold?" If not for his body heat, the furs, and the smoldering fire that burns low in the center pit, I'd be freezing.

"We are accustomed to the weather here, and our bodies have adapted to maintain a certain level of warmth, even during the fiercest cold-dust storms. I also have a beautiful mate to keep me warm." He hugs me tighter.

My face heats at the compliment, but I focus on the other part he said. Storms? Like a blizzard? I shudder just thinking about it. "Can I just tell you I am not looking forward to this cold dust you all are talking about."

"It only lasts for perhaps one of the three lunar cycles of the cold season. Then the warm season will be back."

A whole month of snow? I breathe in. *You can do this.* I've survived escaping to another planet in another galaxy, two Krijese attacks, and moving into an alien village. If I can do that, I can survive three months of cold weather, of which one entire month involves snow.

"Do you think the Krijese up in the mountains will be all right during the cold season? I know you said that the hunting is plentiful, but it has to be a lot harder to find animals when it's cold. Don't they find places to hole up until it turns warmer?" At least that's what I recall from watching old Earth vids about the animals that used to roam. They'd hibernate during the winter months and not come out again until spring.

"The Krijese have been surviving on this planet as long as the Tavikhi. They have also learned to adapt."

I don't know why I can't get them, especially the children, out of my head. Maybe because they remind me of those that live in the bottom tier and who have no one to help them. "What happens next?" It's best to lay everything out in the open, I suppose. He shifts and I tip my head up so we're looking at each other. "Between you and me, I mean?"

He reaches up and brushes my hair gently off my cheek pushing it behind my shoulder. "Whatever you would like to happen."

"That's not an answer."

Zydon runs a finger along my jaw. "It is the only answer I can give you. You are my mate, Remi. The female that Deeka has blessed me with. The goddess says we are meant to be together. That is enough for me. But I know that it is not enough for you. If it were up to me, you would leave the tent you share with your tribe sisters and spend the rest of our lives in my furs. It is not up to me though."

Wow. Okay. "Maybe we could spend some more time getting to know each other."

I sense Zydon's disappointment although there's no evidence of it on his face. "If that is what you wish, then I am glad to give you whatever will make you happy."

Man, why do his words make me feel like I kicked a puppy? "You should be happy too. This isn't just about me. It's supposed to be about *us*."

"If you are happy, then I am happy. All I want is to see your smile and hear your laughter," he says, and it sounds weirdly sincere.

I guess if we're going to get to know each other, we might as well start now. "Why don't you tell me about your brother? The one that is missing. That is, if you want to."

Zydon lays his head down with a sigh and hugs me closer. "Zedam is younger than Zander and me by three warm seasons. He and Zander are the most alike. They take after our baba, while I am more like our nene. Even with our differences, the three of us are close. Especially after our parents passed onto the lands of Deeka."

He's quiet a moment, like he's remembering not only his parents, but also his missing brother. I rest my palm on his chest so Zydon's heart beats strongly beneath it.

"At the start of the warm season, Zedam went out hunting. Most hunters go in pairs. Not only to bring back more kills, but because of the increased attacks by the Krijese. Except that morning, my brother went out alone. He was seen heading through the forest that leads toward the human settlement. When he had not returned by the evening meal, a search party was sent out. They returned just as the first moon was cresting the horizon with only his Krijese-blood-stained sword."

I can't imagine how difficult that has been for both Zydon and Zander. "I'm sorry you lost him."

"Although Zander believes him to be with Deeka, my heart tells me he is still alive," he says with conviction. "Somewhere out there, unable to return to our village for some reason."

"What makes you think that?" I raise my head and rest my chin on the hand lying on his chest.

"Zander and I might be womb mates, but Zedam and I were just as close. My soul would have felt it if he'd traveled into the lands of Deeka."

What would it be like to have Zydon care that much for me? The way Zander cares for London? My parents certainly never did. I want to find out more than anything. I slide up and kiss him. "If you think he's still alive, then I hope one day we find him."

Someone slaps on the outside of the tent.

"Sorry to interrupt whatever you two have going on inside there—you better be ready to spill all the details though, Remi—but Zander is calling all tribespeople to the central fire," Zara, whose voice I'd recognize anywhere, calls through the hide barrier.

With a groan and heated cheeks, I smack my forehead against Zydon's chest. He chuckles, which vibrates through me. She's one of my best friends, but there are days I could strangle her. Slowly, I untangle myself from his arms and from beneath the furs.

"Come, *keeshla*." He stands and helps me to my feet.

I tug down my shirt, which had risen to expose my belly. When I lift my head, Zydon is staring at my waist with dilated pupils. Beneath the fabric, my nipples pebble from the heat in his gaze. Which only draws his eyes up to them.

Playing with fire, I reach up to throw my hair in a messy topknot again since it's a tangled mess, which makes my shirt rise up again.

Zydon scans me from waist to breasts before meeting my eyes. He steps toward me and my breath hitches, but I remain frozen in place with my arms above my head. His hands replace mine and he finishes tying my hair while my arms drop to my sides. My chest pounds and my pulse races. Between my legs, I'm wet and throbbing.

Once he finishes, he tugs my shirt down, and the backs of his knuckles graze my belly. A shiver skims across my neck to rush down my spine. Zydon tips up my chin and kisses me.

"You make me want to ignore my brother's decree and do nothing more than stay in here with my beautiful mate," he murmurs against my lips.

"But then he might send someone to get us," I whisper against his.

"And that would be bad, because then I might have to meet the warrior in the arena and teach them a lesson about disturbing a male and his *keeshla*."

I giggle at the image. "That *would* probably be a bad idea then."

"It would be worth it."

God, Zydon says sweet things like that it makes my belly flip in a good way. "We should get going."

He sighs dramatically and I press my lips together to hold back another laugh. To my delight, he not only takes my hand, but he twines his tail around my waist. I love the weight of it. Together, we walk to the central fire where a massive gathering of tribespeople congregate.

It's crazy that this many people live in the village. That Zander and London lead all of them. Zydon guides me to the outer edge of the circle in direct sight of his brother who stands on one of the backless benches where we eat. His gaze travels around his people, taking everyone in.

His gaze pauses on Zydon and me and a small smile flickers at his lips. He briefly bows his head before moving on. That fluttery sensation returns. It's like he's giving a stamp of approval on his brother's and my mating. I swell with pride. Since coming to Tavikh, I've been given all the things I always wished for back on Earth. People who actually care about me. Who treat me with kindness and respect and love. I have friends and a new family that includes a possible mate. Tears threaten to spill at how happy I am.

"I have news to share with all of you," Zander calls out and the din of conversation dies out as everyone gives him their attention. "Some of you may have already heard, but on a scouting trip today, Zydon and Remi discovered the whereabouts of a small village of Krijese up in the hills."

Gasps and loud murmurs follow. People shuffle their feet, and I catch several females clutching their children close.

Zander raises his hand, and everyone quiets again. "We have spoken to them and they have defected from King Armik's rule. They want nothing more than peace. Which we shall grant them."

His gaze travels again, pausing on warriors as he goes. "No hunter or warrior will greet them with aggression unless they engage first. There is the possibility that their former king will send his warriors to attack. We will offer them the same protection we offered the humans if they want it. Enough of all our people have died."

The tribespeople share looks. It's pretty obvious some of them don't agree with Zander's decision. One of the humans steps forward.

"We came here because it was supposed to be safe. Now you're telling us that more of those killers are just over there." He points in the direction of the hills. "We might as well have stayed back in the settlement. At least we were within four walls instead of out in the open like this."

Zara jumps into the inner circle and glares at the guy with her hands fisted at her sides. "And look how well those four walls protected you. If they were that safe, then you all wouldn't be here. At least here, you have skilled warriors to defend the village. To defend *you*. Your families. They have given all of us food, shelter, and protection without asking for anything in return except doing our part in making the village thrive. Talk about being selfish. Shame on you."

Inside, I'm cheering, because my friend said what all five of us have been thinking. Zydon lets loose of my hand and his tail drops from my waist as he carefully shoulders his way through the crowd. When he reaches the bench where Zander is, he climbs atop it to stand next to him. Seeing him up there supporting his brother gives me the chills. Especially when he addresses the crowd.

CHAPTER 17

"I have been to the village in the hills your shefir speaks off," I call out to the tribespeople. "I have spoken to one of their leaders. Seen the people who live there. They are few, and they are starving. There are only a small number of males, and an even smaller number of females. Two kits also live amongst them. Like us, they only want to protect their tribespeople. We have nothing to fear from those who have made their home near here. They want the same peace we do."

Jodah steps into the circle and glances around. "Zydon and our shefir speak the truth. I have witnessed two of the Krijese while out hunting. They did not draw their weapons on us despite Zydon and I both having ours drawn. I stand with the shefir and will not wage war on their village."

He sets his fist over his heart and bows his head. Benham slowly comes forward and stops in front of us. Out of all the Tavikhi, he has the most reason to hate the Krijese. They slaughtered both his baba and nene. Beside me, Zander tenses. Benham is as close to being a brother to Zander as Zedam and I are. He turns to face the rest of the tribespeople.

"Djentar was a great Shefir. Wise in his counsel. Fierce with his anger. Careful in his decisions. He always put the best interest of his people first, even when not everyone agreed with him." He glances back at my brother and returns his attention to the crowd. "Zander has proven himself to be just as good as, if not better, than his baba as our shefir. This world is changing. Not always for the better. But I swore my loyalty to Djentar and doubly so to Zander. Which means I trust him to see us on the right path."

Benham—who has said more words just now than I have ever heard him speak at one time—pivots to face my brother and slams his fist against his chest. I can sense all the tension releasing from Zander. His worry over whether our warrior brother would support him was for naught. One by one, more warriors and hunters come forward, and they, too, fist their chests and bow their heads until every last one of them is crowded within the central circle. I turn to Zander, fist my chest, and pledge my respect. He returns the gesture and then faces his people.

"Thank you for your trust. If anyone has any more concerns, I am willing to discuss them after the evening meal," he says.

I jump down and search for my mate. My gaze does not have to travel far, because she steps out from between two tribespeople. I close the distance and she takes my hand. We stand there as the tribespeople break away and everyone resumes their daily tasks. Zander and his shefira, along with my *keeshla's* three other tribe sisters, approach.

"You were amazing," Remi says to the one with hair similar to ours, whose face brightens in color. Zara, I believe. These females are important to my mate so I will learn their names.

"Hell yeah, she was," the healer's apprentice—Sage —adds.

Maeve, who is the tiny quiet one, doesn't say anything, but she squeezes Zara's hand.

"You always say what I wish I could." London bumps her shoulder.

"Thank you for your words, brother," Zander reaches out and claps my forearm before turning to Zara. "And yours, my tribe sister."

"People who don't appreciate everything you've done for them piss me off," she says fiercely. "I, for one, am grateful."

"Change is difficult for some," my brother says. "I understand their fears and will do what I can to reassure them. Now, let us all eat and enjoy the evening."

Remi and I trail everyone. She leans into me. "You were pretty amazing too."

I glance down at her and am in awe of my mate's beauty and kindness. "I only spoke the truth."

"Yes, but it is *how* you spoke, not just your words. There was compassion that not a lot of people have, especially for those they don't feel deserving. The universe needs more of that."

"Perhaps together, we can teach this to others."

Remi clutches my arm and rests her cheek against it. "I'd really like that."

My heart soars at her words. We get our food and sit with Zander, his shefira, and all her tribe sisters. I glance at the seven of us and send a prayer of thanks to Deeka for bringing the human females to Tavikh. Kits chase each other around while their nenes try and corral them to eat. My gaze turns to Remi. I try to imagine what our kits would look like. Would they have her dark hair? Or maybe her nenuphar-bud colored eyes? Will they be as fierce and strong as their nene? Will they be tailless or will we spend the warm season learning how to scale the trees?

That reminds me that one day soon, before the cold dust comes, I need to take my *keeshla* up into the trees. She was in awe of the view from the hilltop when we were out scouting. There is a place not far from here, high up the trees on one of the hilltops, where, on a sun-filled day, one can see all the way to the ujera that is a seven-turns-of-the-suns' walk away. The water sparkles like the stars in the sky. It is a place that has clearly been touched by Deeka. I have never seen anything more beautiful—aside from my mate—in my thirty-five warm seasons. She will love it.

"You're awfully quiet," Remi says softly.

I turn to her. "I am just thinking."

"About anything in particular?"

My lips curl. She is still unsure about our mating. I do not want to scare her away by speaking of kits. "Us. Our future. All things a male who has finally found his mate thinks of."

Remi's head barely moves up and down and she returns to her meal as do I. Her tribe sisters, along with the shefira, keep the conversation going. My mate, on the other hand, is quiet. I hope she is giving thought to our mating and the same future I had been thinking of. In this, though, I shall be patient. My mate is worth it. I will work hard to get her to fall in love with me. That is what Zander has done with his *keeshla*.

Once we have finished, my brother turns to me.

"I would like to speak with you and Benham about the warriors' training. The younger warriors need more work if they are going to be ready in case the Krijese strike. I fear their king will disregard any peace treaty offerings he made. Not only because I required the human settlement be included, but also because his own people have left. He will see that as a great betrayal. Did the tribespeople you met give any indication that he is aware of where they chose to settle?"

I think back to the conversation I had with their leader. "Not that I can recall. He merely said they came here for peace and for the plentiful hunting grounds. However, there were enough members of their tribe there, they could not have kept their leaving a secret. It is most likely King Armik had them followed and is well aware how close they are to our village."

Zander remains silent a moment longer. "I believe you may be correct. Which means Benham, you, and I must work on a strategy quickly."

"When?"

"Before we retire for the evening. We will start new training tomorrow," Zander says.

A glance around the fire confirms Benham has already left. As have a few of the tribespeople. The rest linger to clean up, including several humans, and the kits race around after each other. "Let me locate him."

I turn to Remi. "Will you be all right if I leave for a moment?"

"Of course."

Unable to resist, I kiss her quickly and leave her with her fingers over her lips to find Benham. I make toward his dwelling first, but as I pass the weapon stores, he exits.

"Greetings, brother." I lay my fist on my chest, and he returns the gesture. "Zander would like us to meet back at the central fire and work out a strategy for training the younger warriors in preparation for any attack by King

Armik's people. He believes the king will take his anger out on us or his former tribespeople for defecting. Especially as our village stands between him and theirs."

Benham nods. "If there is anything the king hates more than weakness, it is betrayal."

"And yet he betrays his own people by starving them enough they leave for a better place."

"We will make sure the warriors—both Tavikhi and human—are ready. And what of your new mate? Will she be joining them?"

My immediate response is no. Remi will stay out of harm's way. But as much as I wish otherwise, my *keeshla* has a warrior's heart. If I try to take away the one thing she loves, it will break. "If she wishes."

He grunts. "The humans are weak and useless. They have no skills and do not want to bother learning. Your mate is a rare exception."

Pride fills me. Benham does not say anything he does not mean. "My mate *is* fierce, is she not?"

"Tomorrow, I will bring the sword I have been crafting for her. All good warriors need a properly fitted one," he says.

I blink in surprise. "You made Remi a sword?"

"Aye. It is similar to the ones I made for you and your brothers. I'm sure you will teach her to wield it well."

Only Zander, Zedam, and I have specially crafted swords by him. "Thank you, brother." I grip his forearm.

"Come, let us speak to Zander so we can return to our warm tents for the evening." We turn and walk back to the central fire where my mate awaits.

CHAPTER 18

I glance around the slowly dying fire at all my friends and the few remaining tribespeople now that the meal has finished and the sun has nearly disappeared behind the hills. London and Zara are nearby playing Pebbles with Talek and a few of the other children. Their laughter and Talek's trash talk I'll bet money he learned from Zara make me smile. Sage and Kyler have their heads together, probably talking about healer stuff. Maeve snuck away a while ago and went back to our tent. I hope the longer we're here, whatever ghosts are chasing her will disappear.

After making sure I was okay where I am, Zydon moved to the other side of the fire with Zander and Benham to discuss tomorrow's warrior training sessions. What a day this has been. To think that, when I woke up this morning,

I'd only been heading out for a simple scouting trip. Now, I'm sitting here with an alien mate who keeps glancing in my direction and sending me heated stares that have me shifting with awareness. I keep replaying all the kisses we shared earlier in Zydon's tent.

A chill wind blows through and sends air down the back of my shirt, making me shiver with it. I turn my nose up to the air and try to smell the cold dust he mentioned this morning, but the sweet, pungent scent of the burning fire overpowers anything else. A noise brings my head back down.

Zydon has broken off from Zander and Benham and comes my way. His tail swings behind, and I take in the rest of him. The lithe way he moves. His yellowish-white hair swept back off his forehead to billow behind him as the wind hits. Those feline eyes boring intensely into mine. Another shiver runs through me that has nothing to do with the cold and everything to do with the male who settles beside me.

Strong hands wrap around my waist, and I yelp as Zydon lifts me off the wood bench and plops me across his lap. Before I can even try to move, his tail pins my thighs down and his arms envelop me.

"What are you doing?" My voice is breathless.

"I am warming my cold mate," he says it like it should be obvious.

I open my mouth to argue, but Zydon's right. So, I snuggle a bit closer and lay my cheek on his shoulder to absorb more of his heat. "Thank you. I was cold."

"It is always my pleasure to provide you with whatever you need."

I'm actually starting to believe him. We sit together on the bench in comfortable silence. My gaze pauses where the small group still plays Pebbles. A thought occurs to me, and I blurt out my question before I stop to think about it.

"Do you want children?"

Zydon is silent a bit longer. "Like a mate, I had resigned myself to never having kits. It was one more thing I didn't want to hope for, only to be disappointed. It used to be a dream of mine when I was younger though. Having a mate to love. Kits to teach how to be warriors and hunters."

He pauses as though picturing all those things.

"What if you had girls?" I ask. "Would you still have taught then to fight and hunt?"

"If they wished. I would do what made my kits happy." He dips his head, and I lift my eyes to meet his. "What about you, *keeshla*? Do you want kits?"

"It wasn't really something I gave much thought to," I admit. "Mostly because having children meant having a husband—a mate. And there was no one I was even remotely interested in having fill that position. Especially not the man my parents picked out for me."

Zydon jerks and his brow ridges slope upward. "You were to be mated?"

"They tried to force me to get married. He was almost twice my age and was only doing it so he could form a business partnership with my father. He didn't care anything about me." I shudder remembering the creepy way his gaze would linger over my body. So maybe there was one other reason he was doing it.

"It is no wonder you left Earth. I am sorry for what you went through."

I lift and lower my shoulder. "It doesn't really matter anymore. I ran—escaped really—and boarded a spaceship that took me millions of miles away from them and him. It brought me here, where I have friends and people who actually care about me…Remi. They didn't even know who Remington Alcott was. I didn't have to worry they were only pretending. It's been the best thing to happen to me."

Zydon lifts my chin up. "It is the best thing to happen to me as well."

I stare into the eyes I'm coming to love and rise up to kiss him. His lips are soft beneath mine. I twine my arms around his neck and thread my fingers through his silken hair. My nipples harden and heat builds deep inside me. Beneath me, a hardness grows long and thick. Unconsciously I shift, and it slots right between my thighs. I bite back a moan, while Zydon groans into my mouth, and I feel a sort of feminine power I've never felt before. Raucous laughter breaks us apart. He rests his forehead against mine and our breaths mingle.

"It's getting late. I should probably go to my tent." Except a part of me doesn't want to.

"That might be wise. Otherwise, I am not sure I can restrain myself from throwing you over my shoulder and taking you to mine," he whispers gruffly sending a ping of arousal through me.

I swallow and lift my head. Blistering heat pours from Zydon's eyes. Without taking them off me, he unwraps his tail, dragging it achingly slowly across my legs. Despite the pants I wear, it's as though I can feel the buttery softness of it directly against my skin.

I grow wetter. Enough that I worry it will soak through and dampen his clothes. I clench down on nothing.

Finally, I'm free of his embrace and I get to my feet. Zydon stands, making me feel tiny against his height, something no human man has ever been able to do. He takes my hand—his tail once again wrapping around my waist—and walks me through the fading daylight to my tent. When we reach the entrance, he sweeps me up in his arms and claims my lips in a fever-blistering kiss. His tongue plunders my mouth, sweeping alongside mine like a tidal wave crashing against the rocky cliffs I once saw in an old vid.

Someone coughs from inside a nearby tent and brings us both back to our senses. Zydon draws back, but it's with obvious reluctance.

"I will think of you tonight when I am in my furs, my *keeshla*."

His words bring naughty images of our limbs tangled together as our naked bodies glide over one another's. My breathing grows shallow and my pulse races. Before I collapse into a puddle at his feet, I tug the door flap open and step through. I stop with one foot in and twist to partially face him.

"I'll dream of you as well." Before he can reply, I quickly enter the rest of the way and let the hide covering close behind me.

I stand there with my ear pressed against it. Zydon groans low and then his footsteps fade away. I let out the breath I'd been holding. The fire has been banked and burns steadily in the deep pit, giving off a bit of light and heat. A lump lies beneath the furs of Maeve's pallet and soft snores come from it. Careful not to wake her, I cross to my section of our little home and get my sleep clothes from my chest.

I tug my hair out of its knot and run the brush through it before quickly braiding it to keep it from getting tangled while I sleep. The brush gets tossed back into the chest, and I slip out of my hunting clothes. I've just pulled up my loose pants when the door covering opens and Sage and Zara walk through. They both jolt and blink.

"What?" I ask softly.

Sage moves to her pallet and flops onto it while Zara shakes her head. "Nothing. We're just surprised to see you is all."

She sits on her bed closest to the door and removes her shoes.

"Why would you be surprised? I live here, remember?"

"Considering you spent a significant amount of time in Zydon's tent earlier tonight, and the fact that the two of you were sucking face out at the fire, I guess we assumed you'd be with him," Zara explains.

My entire body heats. "We weren't sucking face."

Sage snorts and Zara side-eyes me.

"Okay, fine, so maybe we were. That doesn't mean I'm automatically going to go sleep with him." *You wanted to though.*

"Why not?" Zara asks. "You're mates."

My gaze bounces back and forth between the two of them and I hesitate. Why *am* I not in there with Zydon? *Because you're still not sure if you can believe it's real.*

Zara stands back up and walks the short distance between us. She takes my hands in hers and squeezes lightly. "It's okay to be scared."

I jerk that she read me so well. Then again, she and I come from the same kind of place. With the same kind of parents. The same kind of life. Which really wasn't one at all.

"What if I wake up tomorrow and find out this has all been a dream?" I whisper.

She laughs quietly. "Then this is some psychedelic dream you're having. I mean, smoking hot lavender aliens with bulging muscles and naughty, wicked tails living on a primitive planet? No one can dream that kind of shit up."

I press my lips together so I don't burst out laughing, and Sage chuckles from her pallet. "Yeah, what kind of person would dream traveling to a new planet with super sexy aliens warring with creepy, killer aliens with razor teeth?"

"Exactly." Zara nods with a smile and then grows serious. "Don't let them win. All those people back home? They tried to smother us, douse our flame, but we're too strong for that. *You're* too strong for that."

Tears make my vision blurry, but I blink them away. I take a deep cleansing breath. "You're right."

She scoffs. "Of course I am."

I throw my arms around my friend and hug the crap out of her. "I love you."

"All right. All right. No need to get all handsy." Zara gently pushes me away, and even though she always acts uncomfortable with physical affection, I think she secretly likes it. "Save it for your husband."

Her words startle me and then warmth spreads throughout my body. Zydon *is* kind of my husband, isn't he? The fact it doesn't freak me out more should freak me out. Except…it doesn't. I glance around the tent I've shared with the three of them since we got here. It feels like much longer than a week. A tiny wave of grief hits, because I'm almost certain this is the last time I'll call this place home. But maybe my home is with Zydon now.

"Tell Maeve I'll see her tomorrow, will you?"

Sage nods. "Of course."

I grab a fur from my pallet and wrap it around myself before I step outside and head toward my fate.

149

CHAPTER 19

Leaving my *keeshla* was the hardest thing I have done. For a few beats of my heart, I had truly considered throwing her over my shoulder and bringing her to my tent where she belongs. But I want her to be here because *she* chooses to be. Because she wants me as much as I want her. Not only in my furs either. I want to lie beside her, hold her in my arms, and share with each other all the secrets and dreams we would only share with a mate.

The heat from the fire warms any lingering chill in the air. I strip off my leg coverings and wash up in the water from the clay basin seated on the low table. Using the cloth beside it, I dry off and climb beneath my furs to stare up at the arched canopy of my tent. From the narrow opening that lets the fire smoke escape, a few stars decorate the darkening sky.

Nene would tell my brothers and I stories about how the brightest one is where the lands of Deeka reside. She said anytime we cast our eyes upon it, know that our ancestors are looking down on us. What would they think of my mate? Baba would be impressed with her fighting skills. Nene would no doubt wrap her in her arms and offer her the love and affection Remi never received from her own nene.

A scratching at the entrance has me lifting my head. When it comes a second time, I rise from my furs and push the flap open only far enough to see who it is. On the other side stands my *keeshla* with a fur wrapped around her. She smiles uncertainly.

"Hi," she whispers and clears her throat. "Can I come in?"

I jump into motion and widen the opening. "Of course."

She steps past, and I let the flap close, bringing with it only the light burning off the fire. She turns to face me. Her eyes widen, she makes a high-pitched noise, and promptly spins around, giving me her back.

"Um, you're naked." Remi's voice is a choked whisper.

I glance down at myself and back up. "This is how I sleep."

"Well, yeah, I guess I just expected you wouldn't answer the *door* that way."

A smile curls my lips. Not at her discomfort, but at the slight reprimand in her tone. "Do you not want someone else to see my body? Because it belongs to you?"

She sputters. "That's not what I said."

I move the short distance between us and lean down to brush a soft kiss on her ear. "My naked flesh is only for you, *keeshla*."

Remi shudders at the touch and fiercely clutches her tiny fingers around the fur she wears like a battle cloak. "Yes, well, if I am your mate, then that's the way it should be."

I drag my finger along the back of one hand that holds tightly to the covering around her. "Why are you here, *keeshla*?"

She swivels her head and her gaze drops to my lips, so close to hers. Her small tongue flicks out to wet hers and she raises her eyes to meet mine. Her sun-shaped colored centers are dark in color. Far darker than they are during the day.

"I'm here because," Remi rasps out in a harsh whisper and swallows. "I'm here because *you're* here. And wherever you are is where I'm meant to be."

I close the short distance and lightly brush my mouth across hers. She pivots on her feet and rises up to deepen the kiss with her fingers still clutching tightly to the fur. My hands find the outer swell of her hips and rest there. Just lightly, my blunt claws squeeze, and she whimpers into my mouth. I pull her into the safety of my arms and deepen the kiss.

My mate's breathing speeds up to match the racing of my heart. Never have I known such sweet agony as my *keeshla* in my arms. Gently tugging, I pull Remi's hands off the fur and toss it atop the ones already stacked on my sleeping pallet. I take a small step back and my eyes travel the length of her.

Small pebbles peak her strange, human chest covering, and her sweet scent rises to fill my nose and harden my cock. My nodes swell slightly with mating fluid that soon I'll release inside her to enhance her arousal.

I lift my gaze to meet hers. Remi pulls one side of her lower lip into her mouth and her blunt teeth bite at it. Her eyes shift as though she wants to look away, but my fierce warrior holds my stare as though daring to know what I will do next.

"May I touch you?" It is all I have thought of since the time we spent in our furs today. Perhaps even from before my mating marks appeared.

She loosens the hold her teeth have and her lip slips from between them. Her nod is shaky.

"I want to hear you say the words, *keeshla*. So that there are no misunderstandings between us."

"Yes," Remi whispers harshly. "Touch me. Please."

I glide one hand from her hip up to her waist where the chest covering she wears rises and bares her belly. There is the barest bit of soft, downy hair above and below the small indentation I brush my thumb over it and slide my hand slowly upward, beneath the cloth she wears. Her skin is softer than the slick feathers of the mellenje. At last I reach the fleshy chest mound with its hardened bud.

My entire hand covers and gently caresses it. I keep my eyes on Remi's face so I can tell which of my touches give her the most pleasure. Gently, I roll the rigid tip between my fingers, and her eyes jerk open and a moan spills from her beautiful lips.

"Do you like that, *keeshla*?"

"You know I do," she rasps out.

"I know that your skin has brightened in color and that these tiny pebbles of your chest mounds are hard. I do not know what places on your body bring you the most plea-sure. What places you want me to touch the most. You are the first female I have touched like this. I wish you to teach me what makes you gasp. What makes you moan. I wish to know what will help you reach your release."

Remi tears her eyes from mine, and she stares at the wall of our dwelling. Once again, those blunt teeth dig into her bottom lip. My hand remains where it is. Curled around her chest mound while I wait with far greater patience than I have ever shown for anything.

At last, she turns her head back to me. "I don't know what will. The one and only time I ever did this, it wasn't all that great. It hurt. A lot. And as soon as he got what he wanted, I never saw him again."

Rage turns my vision dark. Some male hurt her? My fierce and loyal mate? "This male forced you?"

Remi's eyes wide and her head rattles back and forth. "What? No. Nothing like that. I knew what I was doing. Well, not necessarily *what* I was doing, but I'd been agreeable to it. I thought he cared about me. Only he didn't. It was fast, at least, and over quickly, thank god. He certainly didn't try to get me to enjoy it."

My whole body is so rigidly held that it aches. I want nothing more than to find a way to go to my *keeshla's* Earth and find all the people who have hurt her and make them pay.

"Hey." Remi's soft palm finds my cheek, and my eyes drop to meet hers. They are soft and filled with a light that shines so bright to almost be blinding. "None of that matters. It's in the past. The only thing I want to think about right now is this. Here. With you and me. When we're together in our tent, no others are allowed. Not even in our minds."

It is as though a dam has been released.

I crash my lips down onto hers. She opens, and our tongues mate in a way our bodies soon will. Together, Remi and I will learn how to bring each other the most pleasure. But I want her to experience it all first. I reach for the bottom of her chest covering and lightly tug. She draws back only far enough that I am able to slide it up and off. My *keeshla* stands proudly before me, looking more beautiful than anything I have ever seen.

"You outshine any goddess."

Remi's lips curl. "You better not let Deeka hear you say that."

"Deeka would agree with me. My mate is perfection. Both inside and out."

She opens her mouth, perhaps to argue, but I claim it with another kiss. I palm her lush chest mound and will my cock to settle until she has found at least one release. Once Remi has lost the ability to speak, I reach for the human leg coverings she wears. She doesn't stop me as I slowly push them down over her hips and the long length of her legs. Between them is a small tuft of glistening wet hair that is the same color as on her head. Her fragrance is strongest there, and I want nothing more than to bury my nose in it and breathe her deeply in.

That bright coloring covers her chest and rises up to her face, but still she doesn't cover herself. I lower myself to my pallet and raise my hand out to her. There's no hesitation. She takes it, and I help her down. We lie on our sides, facing each other. I bring the end of the plait she has her hair in forward and brush the end of it over the hardened tips of her chest mounds. A shudder shakes her body.

I push the plait behind her and run my hand along the slope of her shoulder and down her arm where tiny dots run along the length of it.

"Touching you has become one of my favorite things." I twine my fingers within hers and bring her hand to my mouth, brushing a kiss along each bump.

"*Having* you touch me might just be my new favorite thing." Remi's smile makes my heart swell with joy. "Maybe I can touch you next."

I kiss her hand again. "This first time is all about your pleasure."

She sticks her lips out. "That isn't very fair to you."

"*Keeshla*, I promise that your pleasure will bring me just as much." I lower her hand and slide my fingers along the outside of her hip, drawing a small shudder from her. "Let me show you."

CHAPTER 20

Remi

My entire body is feverish. I should be cold, lying here naked, but I'm about to burst into flames. Zydon's hand, so close to my center, makes my clit pulse and throb. Images of his strange-looking cock won't leave my head. At first glance it resembled the only one I'd ever seen first-hand. But then the differences became more noticeable. Like the raised oblong bumps that line the entire length and reach all the way to the head flared and shaped like an upside down umbrella.

I stare into his eyes and realize he's waiting for my response. Are guys really that unselfish? None of the ones back on Earth were.

You're not on Earth anymore.

I have to keep reminding myself. Tavikhi warriors are different. *Zydon* is different. He's my mate.

"Show me," I finally tell him. "Please."

If I expected him to lose control at my words, I'd be mistaken. Instead, he takes his time, slowly drawing the tips of his fingers along my ribcage, which tickles. My nipples ache with the need for his touch. Zydon traces a circle around the hardened tip. A ping shoots straight to my center. No one's touched my breasts before. I had no idea they could be this sensitive.

I'm glad Zydon's the first. Maybe not the first guy I've had sex with. But the first to show me what intimacy is like. What it's like to stare into another person's eyes and feel closer to them than anyone else in the world. The universe really.

"What are you thinking of, *keeshla*?" he asks in the quiet that's only broken by the crackling fire.

My arms find their way up to circle his shoulders. Muscles dance beneath my fingertips. "How happy I am to be here with you. Not just in your bed, I mean. Just here, in this moment. You make me feel special."

Zydon leans down and brushes kisses over my mouth and then murmurs against them. "There is no one as special as you. You were made for me just as I was made for you."

God, the things he says. His compliments alone could almost make me climax. "You're right. We were made for each other."

That's all the talking I'm able to do because he claims my mouth again. My focus shifts to Zydon's touch. He's everywhere. My arms, belly, breasts. Then his lips replace his fingers. I thread mine through his golden hair as he takes one pebbled nipple in his mouth and locks it between the roof and his tongue. The suction brings my back off the furs, and I press myself closer.

Zydon takes the other breast and gives it the same attention. My cries fill the air. I glance down and watch as he skims down my belly, dropping sweet kisses along the way, until he settles between my thighs. He lifts only his eyes, and they meet mine. His nose is buried in the small amount of hair I have, and he breathes in deeply. More wetness spills from me.

I want to feel self-conscious about his face being *right there*. But the look of pure heat washes it away. No one can fake that kind of need. That kind of want. Zydon doesn't look away when his tongue flicks out to lap up my taste. When he grazes my clit, I nearly buck him off. It's as though a live wire went off inside me.

"You taste like shurup nectar. I could spend all night enjoying your flavor." To prove his point, he devours me.

I can barely catch my breath. His tongue does things I didn't know tongues could do. Zydon doesn't leave an inch of me untouched. It's as though he is trying to memorize every nook and cranny down there. I'm not even mad about it despite the emptiness that grows inside me waiting, nearly begging to be filled. But only by him.

His tongue circles my entrance and then, before I know what's happening, it's inside me. Pushing deep like he wants to drink right from the source. The tension tightens. Then his tongue leaves, and I whine my disappointment. Only it's replaced with pleasure so strong, I keen. Zydon latches onto my clit as though he's done it a million times before.

There's a stretching at my entrance and I realize he's slid a finger inside. I clench down on the intrusion and he groans. My hips rock trying to take him deeper. Slowly, he thrusts the digit in and out before gaining speed. The combination of his mouth and fingers in me is almost too much. I keep chasing something that's just out of reach.

A slight sting and more stretching. I want to focus on one thing, but I can't. The sensations build and my body is going haywire.

"Zydon. Please." My head thrashes back and forth.

"Please what, my mate?" His breath does nothing to cool the raging fire he's started.

"Please." I don't even know what I'm asking for. It's elusive. There's something though. Something just waiting to happen.

His tongue flicks my clit, and an explosion rocks my body. A cry spills from my lips, and my whole body shakes. Tears come to my eyes from the most beautiful sensation I've ever felt. I clutch Zydon tightly to me so I know he's right here with me and won't ever leave.

Finally the tremors wracking my body subside, but electricity still sparks along my skin. He removes his fingers and a shudder trickles down my back. I want to tell him to stay, but he shifts and slowly climbs up until I'm staring into his eyes. His hard length butts up against my sensitive flesh, and I shiver. Zydon brushes the damp tendrils of hair off my sweat-slicked forehead. The tenderness he shows almost brings me to tears again. He treats me like I'm something to be treasured.

"Did that please you, *keeshla*?" he asks softly.

"It was wonderful." And it was. It was perfect. But I want more. "I want you to be pleased as well."

"Everything about you pleases me."

I cradle his face between my palms. "Zydon."

His gaze heats even more and he leans down to claim my lips. I let him in and our tongues slick alongside each other. He rocks his hips and his thick cock bumps against my clit, igniting that spark again. I wrap my legs around him and grind my pelvis upward. The kiss becomes more frantic. Zydon's hands roam, and my fingernails dig into the muscles of his back.

He moves down and slots himself against my entrance, but freezes. I nod. With careful movements, he eases inside, gliding through my wetness. I try not to tense at his size but breathe through the stretch and fullness. He pauses every once in a while and gives me time to adjust, each time kissing me like he'll never be able to get enough of me. That brings more slickness with it, and Zydon inches a little farther in until finally, he's seated fully inside.

"You're incredible, *keeshla*."

I love how rough his voice is. Like it's taking all his control to remain still. Except I want him to lose control. I want him to feel as good as he's making me feel.

"Fuck me, Zydon." The dirty words tumble from my lips before I even know I'm speaking them.

His pupils flare and he thrusts. Slowly at first, and then with increasing speed. There's so much friction and tension. I can barely catch my breath. And then something happens. Warm liquid spreads inside me and little bristles rub my inner walls. A full-body shudder runs from my head down into my curled toes.

"Wha—what's happening?" I stutter and moan with pleasure.

"My mating nodes have opened," Zydon replies in a guttural rasp. "There are tiny hairs within that release a fluid to enhance our pleasure."

I blow out a chuckle. "They're enhancing all right. I don't know if I can take much more enhancing. It's incredible."

He makes to pull away and lock my arms and ankles even tighter around him. More fluid leaks from him, and I gasp. "Don't you dare go anywhere."

His smile is perfect. "My mate likes this?"

"Oh, she more than likes it. I might never let you leave."

"I would not be opposed to that."

I snort. "My friends might come pounding on our door."

Zydon shifts and a small orgasm ripples over me out of nowhere, making me completely forget that I said our. Holy shit. "Move. Please."

He does just that. In and out, going deeper each time. Those little hairs tickle all the right places, and that now-familiar tension builds once again. He reaches between us and fingers my clit, adding more delirious pleasure than any woman has a right to experience. The knot inside me tightens. Sharp breaths and groans fill the tent. I'm sure people can hear us, but I don't care. This is too perfect.

In seconds, it hits. I scream and slam my mouth against his shoulder to try and muffle the sound. Zydon's thrusts grow faster. Harder. Less finessed, like he's also lost to the madness. Fluid fills me that is warm and grows even hotter. Almost unbearably so, but also not. Above me, he throws his head back and roars. The muscles of his neck stretch taut and the gorgeous yellow-gold hair of his cascades down his back, brushing over my hands that hold him tight.

When the tremors stop, Zydon collapses on me, but braces his full weight on his elbows on either side of my head. His hair falls and curtains around us as he buries his face in my neck. The chocolate smell of him fills the air to mix with the musky scent of the two of us combined. When our breathing returns to normal, he goes to his side and brings me with him so we're still connected. I throw a leg over his hips to keep us close.

Zydon presses kisses along my jaw, on my nose, and over both eyelids. He draws his head back, and I open my eyes to meet his. A smile curls my lips. Emotion wells up in my chest threatening to explode out of me.

"My beautiful *keeshla*. My blessing."

"That was so wonderful." Maybe the best thing to ever happen to me. Not just the sex either. Him.

"Yes, it was," Zydon agrees.

"Thank you for making it perfect."

"You deserve perfection."

We lay there in contented silence while he strokes my arm. I almost expect awkwardness to settle between us. I've never laid naked beside someone. But there's a quiet intimacy instead. I trace the mating marks on Zydon's shoulders that have turned almost pitch black. His are shaped and placed differently than all the other mated males of the tribe.

"Do the location of your marks have different meanings? It doesn't seem like everyone's show up in the same place. Or in the same design." Or maybe they're like fingerprints. No two are the same.

"Not that we have found. Although I am not sure I have ever given any thought to it."

I shrug self-consciously. "I sometimes notice random, obscure things."

"Curiosity is a wonderful thing. How else are you to gain knowledge?" Zydon kisses me lightly. "Do not ever be scared to ask a question if there is an answer you do not know."

The tension I'd gained releases. My mother always scolded me for asking too many questions when I was little, so I stopped. I always remained curious, but I no longer voiced questions. Before I can stop it, a yawn escapes.

"Sleep, *keeshla*. Morning will come early and there will be much sparring. Tomorrow, I will show you how to use a sword."

My eyes widen. "Really?"

Zydon nods. "If you wish."

Emotion floods my heart. It feels a lot like love.

CHAPTER 21

ZYDON

My mate sleeps peacefully with her legs entwined between mine and her dark hair splayed out on the furs behind her. I had taken it out of its plait because I wanted to see it spilling down around her. We woke once in the middle of the night with my chest pressed to her back and my cock nestled between her thighs. She opened herself up and reached for me. I slid into her from behind and my tail played with the small nub of pleasure at the top of her sex until she cried out my name and fell asleep in my arms again.

The fire has burned down and there is a slight chill in the air. Faint light shines through the opening above and the low din of activity outside our tent reaches me. I could lie here all day with Remi, but Benham awaits me in the training arena. With the newest possible threat of attack from King Armik's people, we need to be prepared. While his numbers have decreased, they are still a formidable foe.

My mate shifts and stretches with a soft groan. Her eyes flutter open, and a beautiful smile appears on her face.

"Good morning, *keeshla*."

"Morning." She winces slightly.

"You are well?" Was I too rough with her?

Remi's cheek color darkens, but she nods. "Never better. Maybe a little sore, but nothing that won't be gone once I get up and moving."

A rumbling sound comes from her, and she slaps a hand over her belly. The sight makes me chuckle. "Come, let us wash and dress so we can head for the morning meal. Benham is most likely impatient for our arrival."

We rise, and while my mate washes, I add more wood to the fire to take the chill out. I'm finished washing just as she finishes dressing.

"I need to head back to my tent and change clothes," Remi says. "I'll meet you at the central fire?"

As much as I don't want to be parted from her quite yet, she is right. I wrap my tail around her and pull her to me. "I shall miss you."

She lays her hands on my chest and laughs. "I'll see you in fifteen or twenty minutes."

"I do not know how long that is, but it is still too long of a time." I bend and take Remi's lips with mine.

The kiss is long and sweet, and if we both were not needed elsewhere, I would strip her of her coverings and take her back to my furs. Finally, I release her, and she stares up at me with drowsy arousal-filled eyes. She blinks and her vision focuses.

"I'll see you soon," she says and I let her go out the door.

Quickly, I bring out a pair of leg coverings from my chest. From my weapons chest, I grab my sword and sling a sack across my body in case we run across any small game. With my staff in hand, I make my way to the central fire. The fragrant woodsy scent of the morning meal fills the air. I pass several hunters on their way out of the village, as well as warriors ready to head out on patrol, and fist my chest. They return the gesture with a sharp nod. A few humans wander around, each with a clear destination in mind.

I am glad to see them leaving their tents and finding their place in the village. I've had my concerns about them blending well with the rest of our tribespeople—aside from my *keeshla* and her tribe sisters—but I have promised Zander I will learn to be more tolerant.

Benham has already seated himself near the fire to eat. The humans are terrified of him. Most likely not only because of his scarred features, but his gruff personality. He chooses not to speak unless he has something to say and more often than not, it is nothing but rough commands. Benham respects strength and courage. Traits which appear to be rare in humans aside from the few exceptions. He certainly has no love for them.

I help myself to a bowl of grains and take the bench nearest him. Zander should be here soon. Unless he is still caught up in his furs with the shefira. As Shefir, he can get away with it.

"Good morning, brother," I greet Benham.

He nods. A human male approaches the fire and his gaze bounces between the other warrior and me. He swallows but continues walking until he reaches the bowls. The human fills two, and then quickly retreats. Benham shakes his head and makes a noise of disgust.

More footsteps approach along with feminine voices. I turn and my soul light flares to life. Remi, Sage, and Maeve come our way with my *keeshla* in the lead. All three have furs wrapped around their shoulders, while my mate also carries her staff. I rise to greet them. Benham remains seated, but his assessing gaze takes them in. He misses nothing.

"Greetings, tribe sisters." I nod and pull Remi to me as soon as she is within reach. "Greetings, mate."

"You just saw me." She laughs.

"And yet I missed you still."

Remi shakes her head and gives me a quick kiss. "I'm starving."

I release her so she and her tribe sisters can fill their bowls. Sage and Maeve move to the opposite side of the fire than us while my mate comes to me. The sweet scent rises from her bowl of grains.

"The shurup nectar is my favorite too." I gesture to her meal.

My mate glances down at her food and back up. "It's the closest thing to the maple syrup we had back on Earth. There may be a lot of things about the place that I don't miss, but sweets are not one of them. Maeve took us back to the bizele crop the other day and let us taste one. They were delicious, and I may sneak back there again before they're all picked and help myself to another one."

I smile at her. "That was my favorite growing up as well. Our nene would pick several of them, grind them up, and fill this special grain with it. After that, she would heat them over the fire until the grain became crisp and the berry center would become creamy."

Remi moans. "Okay, I'm going to need that recipe. Not that I have a clue how to cook, but maybe if I ask really nicely, one of the elders might teach me."

"I am sure there will be a tribe person who can help."

A shadow covers us, and we both tip our heads back. Benham towers over us. He glances at me and drags a sword off his belt. One far too small for a Tavikhi warrior, but bigger than one for a kit.

"I do not know a human's strength. If it is too heavy, come see me." He passes it to Remi and walks away without another word.

She turns and stares at me with wide eyes. "Oh my god," she breathes. "Did you have him make me a sword?"

"Sadly, I cannot take any credit for it. Apparently, he has witnessed your sparring sessions and is impressed with your growing skill." If Benham had not already crafted my mate a sword, I would have commissioned him for one.

Remi sets down her bowl, rises with her sword, and moves away from the fire. She holds it in both hands and gently swings the sword back and forth in front of her. There is awe and wonder on her face. My heart swells at the happiness she radiates.

"What the hell was that?" Sage asks from her place across the fire.

"Benham made me a sword," my mate calls out. "How freaking cool is that?"

"Damn. He must think you're really good."

"I don't know about that, but I'm doing my best."

Pride swells inside me. My *keeshla* is wonderful. I stand. "Let us go test it out."

"Hell yeah." She nods rapidly and grabs her staff from the ground as well.

We leave her two tribe sisters and head down to the training arena where multiple pairs of warriors are already sparring. The sun is slowly rising and bringing with it a bit more heat. Not enough to call it warm since the cold season is too close to us, but enough that my mate will drip water—what she calls sweat—from her face.

"The sword is different than your stick. It requires you to be closer to your opponent or whatever prey you are hunting. It is also meant to be held in a single hand. You will need to work on your grip." I withdraw my own sword to demonstrate.

Remi watches me intently, her gaze following my every move as I block and strike against an invisible opponent. She sets her staff down near the edge of the training area and comes back with only her sword. I approach and help her clasp the handle.

"It should not feel heavier than your staff, and you should comfortably be able to reach around and have your fingers overlap."

She checks her grip, raises the weapon over her head, brings it back down, and shakes it at her side. Her gaze meets mine. "It feels pretty good."

I let Remi practice swinging a few times so she can get the feel of it in her hand. At least the skin on the underside of it has already grown tough, so with luck, she should not get open sores like she did with her staff. I move closer but still outside of her range, and she lowers her arm.

"Shall we practice?"

"Yes, please," she says with an excited shake.

After locating two pegs of wood, I cap the tip of both our weapons. She gets into her defensive stance, but it is the one meant for when she uses her stick.

"Like this." I move behind Remi and grip her hips.

She glances over her shoulder at me and smiles. "You're just trying to cop a feel, aren't you?"

I don't know what her human words mean, but from her expression and the way she pushes her tailless end back into me, I can guess. I bend and bring my lips to her ear. "If we were not in the presence of these other warriors, I would cop many feels."

Remi snorts and gives me a quick kiss. Too fast for me to return it. "I'll let you cop all the feels later. How about that?"

"I will count the beats of my heart until then."

Once she is in position, I return to my spot opposite her. "Ready?"

She nods and I move. Each of my movements is slow and precise, giving her enough time to anticipate where my sword will strike and block it. We continue to dance, with me on the offensive so she is forced to defend until she moves with ease and control. I call a halt.

"Now you attack," I instruct.

Remi nods and strikes. As with her staff when she first picked it up, her skills need some improving, but she is doing well with the newest weapon. We continue sparring, our speed increasing as she gains more confidence, until I sense her tiring. The sun is halfway to its zenith, and we have been practicing since the morning meal.

"Let us rest, *keeshla*. You have done well. Before long, you may be ready to go out on a hunt with me."

She wipes the wetness from her face, and it lights up with the most beautiful smile. "I can't wait."

I take her hand. "Come, let us head out for a short patrol along the borders of the village. We will return by the midday meal."

Together we leave the training arena and stop at my tent. I sort through my weapons chest and bring out a narrow belt.

"This was mine when I was a kit." I tie the belt around Remi's waist and slide her sword into the sheath at her hip. "I would like you to have it. And then, perhaps one day, you will give it to one of our kits."

Water fills her eyes. She glances down at the belt and strokes the narrow hide with her fingers. She lifts her head and throws herself into my arms.

"This is the best gift anyone has ever given me. Thank you." My mate draws back and gives me a long, lingering kiss.

"As much as you tempt me, sweet *keeshla*, we should head out on patrol."

Remi stands tall and looks every inch the warrior she is. "Lead the way."

CHAPTER 22

Remi

This has been the best day ever. I walk happily through the village gate with my mate at my side. Every few steps, I stroke the belt he gave me and palm the hilt of my sword. I still can't believe grumpy Benham—who I've come to learn from Sage holds almost nothing but disdain for us humans—made me a damn sword. This is like my birthday and Christmas all rolled into one. I should declare today a holiday.

"Keep your eyes and ears sharp," Zydon instructs as we stride through the open field along the border of the forest. "Look out for any signs that someone has passed this way that isn't one of our warriors. Booted footprints. Crushed bari. Listen for the sounds within the forest. They will tell you many things. Which way the wind is blowing. If the mellenje call to each other, then nothing has disturbed them. Listen for ketri or leburin rustling in the brush."

"What's a ketri?" I know leburin are like alien rabbits, but no one's ever mentioned eating a ketri.

"It is a small, underground-dwelling creature with tiny, beady eyes the color of the fiku trees, and whose body often blends in with the bari if not for its dark stripe. It has round ears atop its head, a short bushy tail, and eats many of the plants that grow near to the ground," Zydon explains. "When I was a kit, I wanted to bring one home as a companion, but our nene forbid it."

"Aww, they sound kind of cute."

"I used to believe so."

I smile at the image of a young Zydon carrying around a little furry animal. The image morphs into not my mate, but a child that resembles him. He has the same long flowing hair and those pretty yellow and purplish-black feline eyes. I glance over and that same tender emotion from last night fills my chest. It's too soon to be love, right? Except why is my heart swelling so big it might burst?

My gaze lifts to the sky. Is there really a higher being up there that brings two people together who never would have otherwise met? A being who says the other person —*alien*—is who we're meant to love? I glance over at Zydon. Our first interaction replays in my head along with every single interaction since, like one of those centuries old movie reels.

They've all led us to this moment where I have my own sword and he's teaching me not only how to fight, but also to hunt for no other reason than because it makes me happy. How could I not love someone like that?

A hand on my arm brings me to a halt. I open my mouth to ask what's wrong when a second hand covers it. My gaze jerks sideways to Zydon, but he's not even looking at me. Instead, his eyes are trained on the forest and his muscles are tense. I give a jerky nod to let him know I understand, and he slowly lowers his hand to grasp the hilt of his sword.

I automatically tighten my grip on my staff, although I'm far shakier than he is. What does he see? I study the same place where it looks like he's focused, but there's nothing there. His words come back to me. *Listen for the sounds within the forest. They will tell you many things.* I try and quiet my breathing and strain to hear something. Maybe I'll hear whatever it is Zydon does. Except I realize I don't need to because there's nothing *to* hear. Everything around us is eerily silent.

No birds squawk and no branches or leaves rustle. It's as though even the wind is afraid of making noise. That's when I spot movement. Except it's not coming from where Zydon's gaze is laser-focused. It's to the far left of where we stand. Which is the direction we just came from. Flashes of black blend in so well with the black trunk of the trees, it's almost like whatever is there is camouflaged. Sunlight glints off metal.

Oh shit.

"Zydon," I whisper harshly. "To the left. Look."

Just as I feel his body shift slightly in front of me since I'm probably blocking his view, a Krijese steps out of the forest. Then another. Both have their weapons drawn. These are not the same people from the village in the hills. Which means these are the king's people.

"Fuck," Zydon curses. "Remi, come. Now. We need to get to the village. Hurry."

He grabs my arm and we run. I follow right on his heels as we race through the field and into a copse of trees in the completely opposite direction from where we came. It doesn't matter. I trust him to know where we're going. We dodge tree after tree, and with each one, I swear I feel the Krijese breathing down my neck. I try to listen for any sound they're right behind us, but all I hear is our pounding footsteps and me sucking wind.

We splash through a narrow creek as deep as my knees. I nearly fall, but Zydon grabs my hand and drags me upright. He releases the call of the mellenje, and another follows right after. What's more disconcerting is the grunting, yelling, and screaming from inside the village that finally reach my ears. Up ahead, there are tents and the bizele bushes I recognize. We're coming in the back door apparently.

A roar comes from far too close behind us, and it sends a chill racing down my spine. In one fluid movement, Zydon spins with his sword drawn and drags me behind him as sparks fly when he blocks the strike of a Krijese axe. I nearly tumble to the ground but regain my footing.

"Remi, run," my mate roars.

I'm frozen, my mind returning to the night of the attack on the human settlement. A battle cry jerks me back to my surroundings. Hell no. I'm not going to let these bastards hurt my family. My gaze lands on the second Krijese who slowly approaches—axe drawn—with his black eyes glued on me. His mouth slit opens in what could be a vicious smile.

My fists tighten around my staff, and I walk backwards, carefully placing my steps and never taking my eyes off him. I want to check on Zydon, but I have to trust he can take care of himself. He's a powerful and skilled warrior. A guttural sound meant to resemble a laugh erupts from the Krijese stalking me like I'm prey. It adds to the cacophony of the nearby battle going on between my mate and his opponent mixed with the roars and growls and screams coming from the village behind me.

"Do you think that puny stick is going to stop me?" he scoffs and the sound of his voice grates on me. "I will take you back to our village as a prize. Perhaps you will be strong enough to bear my kits."

I nearly gag at the thought. "Go fuck yourself."

He pauses for only a second and then charges with an ear-splitting yell. I thrust my staff up over my head to block the downward strike of his axe and spin, bringing my stick with me and jabbing it into his side. He grunts and is on the move again. The Krijese swings his weapon, aiming for my right side, and I dodge out of the way, but he recovers faster and aims another strike that I try to block with my staff. Except it slips and instead of hooking under the blade, it gets caught.

The Krijese jerks his axe back, ripping my stick straight out of my hands. I grab my sword hilt and drag it from its sheath. My opponent is big. Lumbering. Relying wholly on his strength. Which means I need speed. I'm no match for him physically, but if I can tire him out, I might stand a chance. It's my turn to go on the offensive and try to catch him off guard. I rush him and he barely has time to block me. He's also hindered by the fact his axe blade is still stuck in the wooden staff, making his movements awkward.

My blade hits its mark and a smear of blood appears on his thigh. He hisses and his temper flares because he yanks my stick off his axe and throws it. I have only a second's notice when he comes at me. He swings. I block it, and the vibration travels the length of my sword, making my hand shake.

We perform our vicious dance, neither landing another blow, until I stumble. His blade edge slices across my free arm, and I cry out.

"Remi," Zydon roars, but I can't look at him.

The damn Krijese laughs as blood trickles down my arm and drips off my fingertips. Tightening my grip on my sword, I wait. Which isn't for long. He strikes. I parry. Metal clangs against metal. My wound hurts like a bitch, but I do my best to ignore it. I'm the one getting tired. I've sparred longer than this, but none of the Tavikhi have come at me with the strength this asshole is. Plus, I've practiced maybe an hour on how to use a sword. I'm not skilled enough.

Sweat pours down my face. The Krijese attacks and hits my weapon so hard I can no longer hold onto it. It falls to the ground, and I dive for it, but I'm too slow. The enemy grabs my hair and yanks me against him. I kick and reach back to claw his face, screaming wild obscenities, but nothing I do has any effect on him.

"Let her go," Zydon cries out.

The Krijese jerks us both around, and I scream in pain. It feels like he's ripping my hair out. My mate stands there with a heaving chest, covered in a mix of his own black blood and the green blood of his opponent, who lies face down in the dirt. My captor brings his axehead up to the side of my face. The scent of blood fills my nose, and I flinch at the cool touch of the razor-sharp edge pressed to my cheek.

"Throw down your weapon, Tavikhi," the Krijese commands. "She does not need a pretty face to give me a kit."

He pushes the blade harder into my flesh and the stinging pain followed by a warm liquid sliding down my face says he cut me. My gaze locks onto Zydon's. Fear flashes in his eyes. Calm suddenly washes over me.

"I love you." The minute the words leave my mouth I twist my body, pulling my head away from the blade, and duck.

There's a sharp sting. My hair is still caught in his fist, which I grit my teeth against, but only a heartbeat later, it loosens, and I fall to my hands and knees. My hair curtains around me. A soft thud comes from nearby, and I lift my gaze. A head stares back at me with lifeless eyes. Vomit rises to my throat, and I scramble back.

"Remi. Speak to me." Zydon's arms wrap around me, and I collapse against his chest.

"I'm fine." It comes out in a croak. "I'm okay."

He helps me sit up and quickly scans my body. There's a slight jerk at my shoulder and a tearing sound as he rips the sleeve off my shirt, exposing my wounded arm. He wraps the hide around it, and I hiss at the pain. Zydon freezes.

"It's all right. Just stings like a bitch." So does my face. But I'm alive. My mate is alive. I only hope everyone else is too.

"Come. The battle sounds have died down." He helps me to my feet, and we head past the elders' tents and farther into the village.

Bodies lie scattered on the ground. Mostly Krijese, but a few are Tavikhi and several humans. Smoke fills the air as the ashy remains of tents are all that are left. Children cry. Tavikhi and humans alike are huddled together, but slowly rise from their protective spots.

I scan every face, hoping to find my sisters.

"Remi," someone screams my name.

My head jerks to the right. Zara and Maeve race toward me. I leap out of Zydon's embrace and run to them. The three of us collide in a circle, arms going around each other, reassuring ourselves that we all survived. Echoes of "we were so worried about you" surround us. Finally we all loosen our hold on each other.

"Where are London and Sage?" I glance around with worry.

"They're fine. London is helping Sage and Kyler with the injured warriors." Zara takes in my arm and face. "God, Remi, we need to get you to the healer's tent."

Zydon joins us and he wraps his around my waist. "That is where we are headed."

I turn to him and place my hand on his blood-covered chest. "Go find your brother and the other warriors who might need help. They need you. Zara and Maeve can take me to see the healer."

He hesitates so long, and I can see him warring with himself. I rise up and kiss him. "I'm good. I promise."

Zydon rests his bone ridges against my forehead for a minute and breathes out a resigned sigh. "Go straight to the healer. Please."

"I will."

He draws away slowly, as though he can't bear to let me go, but finally he releases me, and with a lingering glance, he rushes away in search of Zander and others. I turn back to Zara and Maeve.

"My face and arm are killing me."

"Come on," Zara says looping her arm around my waist. "Let's get you to Sage or Kyler and you can tell us what the fuck happened to you."

I let them lead me to the healer's tent, because I'm not sure I can make it on my own.

CHAPTER 23

ZYDON

It has been four turns of the sun since the Krijese attack on the village. King Armik had been one of the many enemies killed during battle. After his death, the remaining few retreated. While there are no guarantees that a new ruler won't emerge, Zander suspects there will be no more attacks. Not even on the human settlement, which is still under our protection. The Krijese suffered heavy losses.

We have cleared away the tents that had been set fire to, and several of the humans have come together to help build new ones, including the shefira and Zara. Our hide supply is almost gone now because of it, so the hunters have stayed out longer, trying to find more game.

We lost three warriors and five humans during the attack and many others were injured. The village has been mourning, but their life celebration last night will help us heal. The shefira, my *keeshla*, Zara, and Sage have been helpful with organizing the people and assigning everyone tasks to rebuild what we have lost. Maeve and Alanda have been preparing some of our food stuff for the cold season.

Remi steps out of our tent and carefully stretches, being sure to keep her injured arm at her side. Ever since the first night she slept there, she has made it her home as well. The mark on her face will heal with time, as will the wound on her arm. She is lucky that it only required a few stitches. Her eyes meet mine and a smile spreads across her lips. My heartbeat picks up the pace.

I close the distance between us, wrap my tail around her, and kiss her softly. "Good morning, mate."

"It definitely is," Remi murmurs against my lips, her palms lying on my chest.

"What are your plans for the day?" Kyler instructed her to refrain from sparring for at least ten turns of the sun. A fact my mate has been unhappy about.

Her soft fingertips trace my mating marks. "I told London I'd meet her later this afternoon so we can work on more inventory and seeing what things we're still short on to get us through the cold season."

Wonderful. This gives us time. "I have a surprise for you."

Remi pulls back. "For me?"

"Do you not like surprises?"

She makes a face. "None of the ones I've ever received before have been that great."

I bring the tail of her plaited hair over her shoulder and stroke its length. "Do you think that I would give you a surprise if it was a bad one?"

Her head tilts. "No."

Giving her my best smile, I unfurl my tail and take her hand. "Come. Let me show you."

Remi grins back and with her fingers threaded through mine, we walk through the village and out the gate.

"Are you sure it's safe to be out here without my weapon?" she asks.

I glance down at her. "We will not go far. I swear I will protect you if need be."

"That's what I'm worried about."

"Do you trust me?"

Remi's elbow nudges my side. "I'm not going to take offense that you asked me that."

"Then trust me, *keeshla*."

She lays her head on my shoulder. "I do."

We make our way along the outer border of our tribe's land, toward the hills, until we reach the one that is our destination. I guide her to the gently sloping path that winds itself back and forth up the side of the hill until we reach the top. We come to a stop at my favorite tree.

I release Remi's hand and leap onto the closest branch to the ground that will hold our weight. She stares up at me and laughs.

"What are you doing up there?"

My tail loops around the branch and I lean down with an outstretched arm. "It's your surprise."

Remi shakes her head with a small laugh but reaches up and clasps my hand. I swing her up with me and hold her close. Our faces nearly touch, and I can't resist kissing her beautiful lips. I give her my back and glance over my shoulder. "Climb on and hold on tight."

Proving her trust in me, she does exactly that. Once I am sure she is secure, I leap to the next higher branch and the next, using my tail to keep us balanced. Remi squeaks the higher we go, but she doesn't loosen her hold on me. Finally, we make it to the top, where there's a perfectly formed seat big enough for us. I lower myself and brace my back against the thick trunk.

"Sit." I separate my legs.

Slowly, Remi takes her place between them, and I pull her tighter against my chest. My arms go around her and I'm careful not to trap her injured limb beneath mine. She leans her head back to rest against my shoulder. Reaching into the bag slung across my body, I pull out the fur I'd brought with and cover her with it. She sighs and snuggles deeper into me.

"Are you warm enough, *keeshla*?"

Remi mumbles an uh-huh and nods. "You make a very nice heating pad."

The sun is nearly at its perfect spot and I'm content to hold my mate tight. "This was one of my favorite places to come when I was a kit similar in age to Talek. I discovered it on one of my first hunts. I'd been chasing after a burracak and got separated from Zander. The creature darted up the tree, and being as impulsive as I was, I climbed up after it. I made it all the way up here without finding my prey, only to realize I did not know how to get back down."

"Oh no. Were you scared?" Remi asks.

"If I say yes, will you think me weak?" I chuckle to show I am making a joke.

She turns her head and draws back so she can look me in the eye. "I would never think you were weak."

I give her another kiss—something I will never get tired of doing—and then return to my story. "I yelled and yelled for Zander. It took him until the sun was well past its zenith to find me. By that time, I had worn myself out and was too tired to try and figure out how to get down. He settled in beside me, and the two of us slept here until we were rescued the next morning."

"I bet your parents were so worried."

"Nene was terrified, and Baba was angry because we had made her worry."

Remi strokes my arm. "I can imagine."

"But the one thing I don't regret was being up here to witness Tavikh in all its glory."

"It's beautiful," she says.

"Not nearly as beautiful as you." At that moment, the sun reaches its peak and I point in front of us. "Look, *keeshla*."

My mate sits upright and sucks in a sharp breath. "Oh my god."

In the distant valley, the sun hits the waters of the ujera, and it sparkles as though a million stars float on top. Every color reflects off it, bouncing off the lush group of trees that surround the body of water. It shines brightly like Deeka herself has blessed the place. Small flakes of cold dust fall around us. Several heartbeats pass, and as the sun moves, the bright light dims until the ujera returns to its regular dark color that blends into the trees.

Remi turns in my arms to face me. She swings one leg to the other side so she straddles my lap. My cock hardens even more as she settles closer to me, and the heat of her core nearly burns. Her arms lie across my shoulders, and she stares into my eyes. "Thank you for bringing me up here. That was the most amazing thing I've ever seen."

"I am glad you enjoyed my surprise."

She smiles, but it quickly turns into something more... seductive. "Oh, I did. And I think you've earned a surprise of your own."

With that, she lays her lips over mine and sweeps her tongue across them. I open for her, and she slicks across the inside of my mouth and grinds her cunt against my hardness. The kiss grows heated, and I palm her ass, dragging her up and down the length of my cock.

Remi scrambles to her feet and yanks off her pants. They drop from her fingers and slide toward the edge of the branch. I grab them before they fall and hook them on another one nearby. She bends and works at the tie of my leg coverings. I help her and shift side to side to slide them down enough that my cock springs free.

In seconds, she is back in my lap sinking down onto my length. Her warm heat surrounds me, and it takes everything I have not to come like an untried kit. The soft press of the hardened buds of her chest mounds grinds into me, and then she claims my mouth with hers.

Once again, my palms grip her hips, and I drag her forward and back, going deeper with each thrust. Our lovemaking is frantic. My tail twines around her and dips down between the crease of her ass. I reach between us and finger the nub at the top of her sex.

"What is this called?" I growl against her lips.

"It's a clit."

"Clit," I repeat, loving the sound of the word.

My tail end glides along the outer edges of where my cock rests inside her, and her wet slickness coats it. I draw it away and encounter her back hole. Remi freezes and our eyes lock. When she doesn't protest, I swirl the tip around the small pucker and mimic the movement with my finger on her clit. She releases a throaty moan and swivels her hips, grinding down on both my cock and my tail, which has barely entered her.

"Come for me, my mate."

Remi continues working herself against me, and I alternate the thrusts of my cock and tail, all while paying attention to the sensitive pleasure center. Tension builds in me, but I hold back until my mate has climaxed first. Her cries fill the air, and with one more swirl of her clit, her back arches and she tenses. Around my cock, she squeezes, and that is all it takes for me to release inside her.

My mate's head drops onto my shoulder, and she breathes heavily against me. Small tremors from inside her cunt still stroke my cock. Remi shivers, and I drag the fur back over us.

"Better?" I stroke her back and she nods against me.

We remain connected, neither speaking, until the sun is almost at the other end of the sky. She raises her head and moves to climb off my lap, but I stop her. Eyes the color of the flowering buds of the nenuphar bush meet mine.

"Before you arrived on our planet, my life was plain. Dull. I had been prepared to live without a mate until I passed onto the lands of Deeka. I almost believed she had forsaken me. But then I met you. It was as though I could see every color again. Life had meaning again. I had a purpose." I palm the uninjured side of her face. "It was to love you, Remi."

"I love you too." She presses her lips to mine in the sweetest kiss.

Carefully, I help her off me, and we both stand and put our coverings back to right. She climbs onto my back again, and I slowly make my way down the tree until we reach level land. Just as she loosens her hold and her feet touch the ground, the sound of a stick breaking comes from far too close. I glance around for a weapon, cursing myself for not being more cautious, when a male with dark mating marks and holding a staff steps from between two trees. He comes to an abrupt halt with his eyes locked on mine. Dark pupils flare, and he jerks.

"Why did you stop so fast?" a muffled female's voice comes from behind him.

She steps around the Tavikhi male who is still staring at me—and I him—but neither of us can look away. I feel my *keeshla* move closer to me, and her small hand slips into mine. My heart has almost stopped beating. And then it races.

"Zedam?" It comes out a harsh rasp.

The female gasps and my brother's eyes close as he takes in a deep breath. Slowly they open again and joy spreads across his face.

"Zydon."

We both move at the same time, closing the distance between us until we are in each other's arms. I squeeze him tightly to me and then draw away to rest my bone brows against his. "We thought you were dead."

"I am sorry for what you must have suffered. If I could have come back to the village, I would have."

At last, we separate, and he holds out his hand for the female still standing there with the water my mate calls tears in her eyes. Zedam brings her to him and his tail wraps around her waist. Remi's arm wraps around mine, and I hold her close to me as well.

"Zydon," my brother begins. "This is my *keeshla*, Eloise."

"I'm so happy to meet you," she says with a soft smile that reminds me of my mate's.

"The honor is all mine, sister." I look down at the female at my side and back to Zedam with so much happiness spreading through me. "Brother. Sister. This is my own *keeshla*, Remi."

She takes a half step forward. "Welcome home. Zander and Zydon have missed you so much."

Zedam fists his chest. "Thank you."

"Come, my brother and sister. Let us go home so we can hear your story and celebrate your return. Many things have changed since you have been gone."

The four of us slowly make our way down the hillside. I have my *keeshla* and now my brother back. Deeka has given me far greater things than I could ever thank her for. Still, I offer her my prayers of gratitude. Remi's hand tightens around mine and I glance down at her. My mate. My love. I have never been more blessed.

EPILOGUE

Maeve

I haven't always been afraid.

Only since David. Months later, I'm not sure how to *stop* being afraid. How I found the courage to hide on a spaceship bound for another planet is beyond me. It still doesn't seem real. Yet, as I gaze around the central fire where aliens and humans alike celebrate the return of Zander's missing-and-presumed-dead brother, Zedam—who is very much alive and *mated*—it's all too real.

I tug the fur tighter around my shoulders to try and ward off the chill from the cold season. I'd be warmer if I moved closer to the weird smelling fire whose smoke always tickles my nose, but that's where all the people are. As a gust of wind blows in my direction, I rub at the itchiness and try not to sneeze while I take in my friends gathered around it.

London is speaking to Eloise, Zedam's mate, who he brought with him when he returned. I'm so happy London has settled into her role here. She was the first person I'd spoken to after sneaking onto the Exodus Voyager. For two months, we were roommates who became close—best—friends. Yet she still doesn't know who I really am. No one does, and I plan on keeping it that way.

London, Remi, Zara, and Sage all know me as Maeve Anderson. The person I used to be—Katherine Waters—died before she ever boarded that spaceship headed for Tavikh.

Zara stumbles over, laughing and carrying a wooden cup, and collapses on the giant log I'm sitting in front of. "Maevey, what are you doing over here all by yourself? You should come join us. They have this *really* good drink that makes you feel all fuzzy inside."

She hiccups and I chuckle. Usually she calls me Maeve or Mae. This is a first for Maevey. "I'll take your word for it. And I'm fine right here, thank you."

She leans down and puts her face right in mine. The fermented scent Zara breathes out almost makes me draw back, it's that strong. She squeezes her eyes shut, opens them wide, and blinks a few times. "Nope, there's still two of you."

"Hey, what are you guys doing over there?" Remi calls from where she stands at the fire with Zydon, whose tail is wrapped around her waist.

"I'm just keeping Maevey company and trying to convince her to give this yummy goodness"—Zara holds up her cup —"a try, but no such luck. She's smarter than us."

That's up for debate.

"Do you want me to bring you some since you don't want to come join us? It's really good."

After David, I'm not a fan of alcohol. I've seen what it can do to people. "How about you drink mine?"

Zara hiccups again and nods. "Don't mind if I do. Thanks, Maevey."

She hoists herself off the log, stumbles a few steps, rights herself—sort of—and rejoins the tribespeople back at the fire. I continue studying everyone. The Tavikhi have been kind to us since our arrival, not just at the village, but also on the planet. Except kindness often hides the darkness. Which means, every day, I wait for the illusion to drop away and for true colors to appear. It's a damn shitty way to live I've discovered.

Sparks fly and wood pops from the fire, making me jump. London glances over and detaches herself from the group. She sits on the ground beside me and lays her head on my shoulder.

"Are you staying warm enough?" she asks in that way she has ever since after the first few weeks of being room-mates. It's soft and quiet so it doesn't draw anyone's atten-tion. She knows I hate having attention on me. I want nothing more than to melt into the background.

I nod even though I'm not. Not really. "I'm okay."

"Whenever you want to sneak away, you can. Don't feel like you have to sit here if you'd rather be in your tent and away from all the people." She lifts her head.

This is why I love London so much. She knows me so well, and not once has she ever pushed me to tell her why I came to Tavikh. She's accepted me without question. In fact, all my friends have.

"I love you. Thank you for being such a great friend."

"I love you too." She hugs me tight and gets to her feet. "Remember what I said."

When I nod, London walks back to where Zander stands. The minute she's within reach, his tail wraps around her and he pulls her close to him like he never wants to let her go. I shudder, and not only from the cold. David was like that. Possessive. Never letting me out of his sight. Getting angry if I talked to anyone else, which I never did. And not only because of him. Being from the bottom-tier caste is mostly about survival, especially if a person doesn't have any family left.

My parents were both gone before I turned twenty. After that, it was working in the factory ten hours a day, trying to make enough money to afford food and rent. Clothes. Medicine. We slogged through though. We had to. It's also where I met David.

I shut down all thoughts of him. He doesn't matter anymore. I'm millions of light years away from him. He can never hurt me again. And maybe one of these days, I'll learn how to not be afraid. I let out a sigh. It's time to go back to the tent I share with just Zara and Sage now that

Remi moved in with Zydon. Once I'm standing, I pull the fur tighter, and then quickly slip away before anyone notices.

It's not that easy navigating in the dark, despite the random torches outside some of the tents. Humans don't see as well as the Tavikhi. And despite being here for over two weeks, it always takes me a minute to get my bearings and head in the right direction. I weave around a few dwellings, and just as I'm passing the healer's tent, a huge, towering figure exits it in a hurry. It happens so fast, neither of us can stop the collision.

I crash straight into a rock-hard stomach and bounce right off it. My fur slips out of my hands as I fall and flail my arms to try and stay upright. Except I don't hit the ground. I'm caught mid-air. A grunt comes from above me and my head snaps up. And up, until I'm staring into hardened yellow and purple feline-like eyes. The nearest torch shines pale firelight over us and the sudden flare of color as the tattoos on his body change and brighten.

No. No, no, no. I don't even realize I'm shaking my head until my hands come up to the massive chest and push as hard as I can. And then the single word echoing in my ears spills from my mouth again and again.

"No. No. No."

He quickly releases me and steps several feet away.

Someone else comes out of the healer's tent, but I can't take my eyes off the warrior in front of me as denial runs through me.

"What's going on? Oh shit." Sage moves between him and me, forcing my gaze to hers. "It's okay, Maeve."

It's not. It's not okay.

"Hey, you're all right. Why don't we head to the tent and get out of this cold? You're shivering." She picks the fur up off the ground, and my gaze goes right back to the warrior who stands rigid and who still hasn't uttered a single word.

Sage wraps it around me and gently tugs me forward and away from him.

"Benham, you should probably go get London, Zara, and Remi," she says over her shoulder as she guides me to our tent.

She grabs the torch from outside it and pulls back the hide flap covering the entrance. "In you go."

Moving on autopilot, I walk in, but I'm not even seeing anything. Am I a bad person? Is this my punishment for something I've done? It has to be. Why else would the goddess the Tavikhi worship decree I'm the fated mate of the most terrifying warrior in the entire village?

Thank you so much for reading! Please consider leaving a review.

Want a sexy bonus scene with Zydon and Remi? Sign up for my newsletter and receive not only the bonus, but you'll also get access to VIP content including early cover reveals, new release information, and you'll stay up-to-date on all things Warriors of Tavikh

Get your bonus scene HERE

Want to know how Zedam and Eloise met? You can find out in Fated to the Lost Warrior. Get your copy HERE.

For Maeve and Benham's story, check out Fated to the Alien Grump

---

Maeve

Fearing for my life, my closest friend helps me get a completely new identity. One that allows me onto a ship bound for a planet light years away from the death that awaits me if I remain on Earth.

Months later, life on Tavikh is good. As long as I avoid the attention of the massive Tavikhi warriors—the alien race native to this planet. Two of my best friends may have found their mates amongst them, but the men—males—terrify me. Especially the largest, grumpiest warrior in the village.

Benham

From the moment the humans arrived on Tavikh, we have done our best to protect them from our enemies. And yet, all they do is take advantage of our shefir's kindness. All except for the new shefira and her four closest tribe sisters.

They bring hope to our people. Or at least to those wishing for a mate. Which does not include me. At least not until I accidentally collide with the smallest, always-frightened female who triggers my mating marks. Now I must prove to her that, with me, she has nothing to fear.

Warriors of Tavikh

Fated to the Alien Warrior
Fated to the Alien Hunter
Fated to the Alien Grump

About the Author

Erin Hale resides in the South where the summer humidity sucks the breath right out of you. She's mom to the best dog on the planet. In her free time, she enjoys reading about swoon-worthy aliens (and secretly wishes one would land on Earth) and monsters alike. She also loves traveling the globe and can be seen most often in any of the pubs in the UK—where the weather is much more acceptable—with a raspberry gin and lemonade in hand.

To stay up-to-date on all her latest news, be sure to join her newsletter <u>HERE</u>!

I'd love for you to join my reader group! You can find us in Erin Hale's Hideaway